A TOM COLLINS TO GO

Jim Hart

Front Cover Photo by Jim Hart
Back Cover Photo by Jim Hart
Author Photo by Chris Hart

The author would like to thank Michael R. Valentino and Bill Rednour for their editorial assistance.
Copyright © 2016 Jim Hart

ISBN: 0692785744
ISBN 13: 9780692785744
Library of Congress Control Number: 2016916043
A Tom Collins To Go, Brooklyn, NY

Dedicated to my producers...

Joseph and Elizabeth Hart

CHAPTER 1
MONDAY, JANUARY 6, 1947

D awn's first rays crept over the city as I rolled my head so my one good eye was facing the windowless wall. Even the glare off the flat baby-shit brown paint reflected the trauma of a new day. Seven a.m. An ungodly hour. Days shouldn't start till noon. Then, maybe four a.m. closing times wouldn't seem quite so bad.

The Woody Woodpecker song came blaring from the radio in the apartment next door. Some dumb radio guy's idea of a funny wake up song. Guess that's why he's riding platters over-nights from a two-bit station at the bottom of the dial instead of spending swinging evenings with the Big Bands from atop some live hot spot.

I drink a little too much. Hell, I'm a drunk. Not like most drunks, drinking to forget the bad day I just had, the lousy dead end job, or even the love lost. I'm different. I drink to remember. I never want a day to go by that I don't think of that miserable ex-wife of mine, Thelma. Ah, the lovely Thelma, who had been making love to my partner for five years before finally having the decency to run off with him, taking with them everything I had, including my modicum of self-respect. He had even kept the Parlor Detective Agency name when he left and opened a bigger, ritzier office in a better part of town.

Some detective I was. "Here's to you, babe, and to you too, Steve Taylor, you no good son-of-a-bitch." I begin each day with the same warm toast, pulling open the small top drawer to my nightstand and hoisting a pre-poured shot of bourbon. No matter how drunk I get the night before, I always remember to pour that shot. I am, if nothing else, consistent. A fact to which most bartenders in the Red Hook waterfront section of Brooklyn would attest. And they could each point to a table, a chair, or a mirror that good old Harry Parker had smashed during one of those nights and come back the next night or a few nights later and replaced. I was consistent in my debts of honor as well. However, if the cases keep coming in, or rather not coming in at the present rate, I may soon be forced to become a much less abhorrent drunk.

I hit forty-five years old with the turn of the new year. No wife, no kids, no clients, and down to about twenty-seven bucks. Not exactly dough heavy. How does someone who was such a smart kid all the way through high school, hell, how does anyone wind up like this? Thelma. Thelma, the married too young, gimme, gimme, get me, get me, blood sucking badger extraordinaire. Thelma of the shimmering hair and serious movie star beauty who, cruelest cut of all, left my money and stole my dreams.

I had spent eight years pounding a beat as a member of New York's Finest only to throw it all away in one unguarded, heated moment of fist meeting face of superior officer because he was trying to fill me in on Thelma's ... indulgences. At least part of that was a crock of shit; Bernie Kaminsky my caustic ex-squad sergeant was trying to taunt me about Thelma, not fill me in and he was never anybody's superior ... at anything.

Enough self-pity, analyzing my wasted life. Another first shot awakening, another day. Thelma and Bernie Kaminsky both be damned. I knew there was no use trying to get back to sleep. No matter how much, or how little I slept, once I was up, I was up. I slipped my feet into my furry slippers, a 1941 Christmas gift from Thelma. She was already screwing Steve when she gave me these, I thought each morning as I shoved my feet into them. I stood and shuffled the six or seven steps to the kitchen area, took out the box of Kellogg's Corn Flakes, which old man Kellogg had long ago promised was a healthy way to start each day, and poured the remainder of what I hoped was still milk from the bottle which stood lonely in the little fridge, one of the few luxuries I had gotten to take from the marriage because Steve had a bigger, better model. I sat at the small round table and took in all of my one room, paint slightly peeling, ceiling slightly leaking, forty-three dollar a month Shangri-La. Some mornings self-pity is harder to shake off than others.

Battle Creek, I read from the cereal box. Sounds like a place where Thelma and I could have lived happily ever after. I started to pour more flakes into my bowl, then remembered that the cow had run dry. I'd go downstairs and ask Mrs. Geetus, my landlady, for some milk, but I knew that would only cost me double in return and when you don't have enough for one bottle of milk you sure as hell don't have enough for two. It was Mrs. Geetus' house policy that whatever was borrowed was replaced twofold. Sweet old lady, Mrs. Geetus. Generous to a fault. The kind of woman who made the local loan shark look like a philanthropist. I went to the sink, shoved aside the pile of dishes with varying degrees of caked on crud, and let the hot water run. I took my old Gillette from the drawer with the knives and forks and pulled the little mirror on its extending gizmo from the wall. As usual, the hot water was somewhere just above the freezing point and my safety blade was dull enough to lend to a four year old without having his mother screaming bloody murder. It was even dull enough to lend to a guy married to Thelma I laughed without fear of cutting myself.

One of the other boarders was coughing his usual early morning hock in the hallway and I looked toward the door. In the stuffed chair next to the door I saw some mail. Mrs. Geetus dropped everybody's mail inside their rooms. She would just walk in with it, stop to say hello if you were in, do God-only-knows what if you weren't. The doors had no locks; not that locks would have stopped Mrs. Geetus anyway. I had once jammed one of the two straight-backed chairs from the table under the doorknob in hopes of keeping some very nasty men who were tailing me from murdering me in my sleep. I awakened to a lecture on the cost of straight-backed chairs from Mrs. Geetus as she stood above me while I fumbled with the covers trying to conceal my nakedness, which she hadn't seemed to notice. And in spite of, or maybe because of, the fact that I couldn't figure out how the hell she got past that chair, I accepted her right of entry from that day forward.

I took a last look in the mirror, at the uncloseness of my shave, and added razor blades to the mental list of things I had to buy as soon as I got a client. I scooped up the three letters from the chair and took them over to the table and sat down. From the return address I saw the first one was from Vincenzo Preetsatori, of Preetsatori's Auto Emporium - 132 Sackett Street. Skinny Vinny, I thought. A bill for the removal of two bullets from, and the plugging up of, the radiator of the old '38 Buick Special. The car wasn't much, but it was all I could afford and I had nursed it through the war years when no cars were being made and it had gotten me around okay, so now I figured I owed it some. Fancyschmancy, we're getting, Vinny, sending bills. You've got the car: you know I have to come pay for it! I threw the envelope aside without opening it. Whatever the going rate for bullet removal was these days I was sure I could argue it down better in person with Vinny. The second envelope, I also knew from the return address, was from Doc Dearborn who had an office, sort of, five blocks east of Vinny's garage. Doc probably could have been a good sawbones if he could have stayed away from old Dewars and young skirts. I knew this was another bill, for the removal of one bullet from my left shoulder, embedded in the same chase up Eastern Parkway that had lost me the use of my Buick and my only brown sports jacket. Doc sent bills to all his patients, not so much as a reminder of monies owed but because it was the "professional" thing to do. And after I had just got that bimbo to stop threatening him about talking to his wife regarding their little tete-a-tete. Well, here's another one better handled in person. I tossed it with the same casual air as I had Vinny's and as fate would have it, it landed right on top of his. It was nice they had each other for company.

The third envelope was clearly from no one I knew. It had the name J.E. Collins and a Pierrepont Street address from the very-very-upper-crust Brooklyn Heights section of town embossed, not written, in a perfectly symmetrical pattern in the upper left hand corner of the envelope. There was no stamp, which meant it had been hand delivered. This one I opened.

Dear Mr. Parker:
    A matter of the utmost urgency has arisen.
    I wish to employ you in this regard.
    Repondez s'il vous plait.
    ESplanade2-3697
    7:30 P.M. This Evening.

        Urgently yours,

        J.E. Collins

Only big bucks spell out R.S.V.P., I thought. He probably had his secretary type it. What a life. She may have signed his name too, the signature looked a bit feminine. Maybe after tonight the shelves won't be the only thing in the old Sears Coldspot refrigerator. I smiled at the thought and started to map out a strategy to use on Skinny Vinny. Even pulling up to the Collins place in my old heap was more reliable than taking the train, I figured. Besides, Collins didn't figure to get a gander at the ... imperfect condition of my car. It didn't seem he'd be the type to be peeking out windows or answering his own door.

I knew this Collins guy must have all kinds of ways of finding things out about people, especially ones he intended to employ, but I didn't like that the letter came here and not to my office, if you could call it that. Syd, of Syd's Candy Store around the corner, had cleared, make that half-cleared, his back storeroom for my use. People who looked me up in the phone book were always confused when they got to the address and found Syd's. Maybe I even lost some clients who didn't bother to come in and ask, but for only eight bucks a month I got to work out cases and meet with clients among the sweet scents of Tootsie Rolls and Mounds bars. Syd and his wife Sarah got a big thrill seeing the people who came to me for help. They always saw me as needing help myself and wondered how I could solve anything. Syd and Sarah took messages from one of the two phone booths in the front of the store. The one on the right was the number I used as my business number. They also took messages from walk in customers and brought them back to me. No extra charge. They were that fascinated by my work. I occasionally soda-jerked or swept up if one of the kids were sick or if Syd was off buying some new exotic sweet just out on the market. I still remember the excitement that came with the arrival of the first case of Milky Ways a couple of years ago. Syd and Sarah shared one, ooh-ing and ah-ing, probably louder than on their six nights of child conception.

Down in the street a car horn beeped twice. The sound coming in loudly through the slightly opened window. Mr. Bellem, who I had heard earlier in the hall, was undoubtedly getting another ride to the post office where he worked as a mailman. "From that younger, married woman," as Mrs. Geetus, who possessed and willingly shared a great wealth of community knowledge, had confided.

My thoughts shifted gears back to the Buick. No con. None needed, just tell Vinny the truth, or part of it anyway. I'll tell him I got a client but I won't tell him what part of town the job's in. That little "entrepreneur" would jack up the price of that radiator so high that a friggin' giraffe would get a sore neck.

I'll just say I got a tail job. Husband messing around. No, wife messing around, Vinny loves to hear about cheating wives, may even knock off a few bucks if I juice it up just right. A blonde, a hotel room, a bottle of bourbon, and of course an Italian lover. Okay, maybe a slight con job was in order.

I checked my watch, a gift from Steve. Two-thirty it lied. It never had told me the correct time. Steve of course didn't know the watch couldn't tell time. He had given it to me, he said, so I could better keep my appointments. So when he told me to meet him at his place at three one afternoon and I walked in at one and caught him and Thelma in a very acrobatic position we were all quite surprised. He had probably picked the damn thing up in a pawn shop or taken it from some poor stoolie he was hustling, promising in return for the watch and a little pocket change not to let the bulls know where the poor schmo was hiding out. Timing, as they say, is everything.

A look out the window to the big Gold Medal Flour clock on the building down the street told me it was ten to eight. This seemed more in keeping with the pounding in my head and the clicking echo of sexy high heels worn by young, long-legged, lovely babes on their way to work.

I had a lot to do before seven-thirty and at the top of my list was a trip to Syd's with a mitt full of nickels, for telephone calls. My first call was to Cudge. Tony, "Cudgel," "Cudge" to his best friends, Congelluno, thirty-eightish, short, fat, black wavy hair and as strong as a Caddy V8, had earned his nickname clubbing guys over the head. Guys who had been stupid enough to borrow money from Patsy "the Shark" Morringello and then somehow developed a case of amnesia when it came time to paying him back. Guys in the neighborhood said that Cudge had proved over the years to be more of an expert on curing amnesia than Freud or Jung or any of those fancy degreed boys. He had never failed to recoup Mr. Morringello's money. Considering some of the heavyweights who borrow money from Mr. Morringello, never is an extremely big word.

Cudge was shy one finger and had suffered a slight shakeup in what was once an excellent brain. He had taken a fall back in '30 while working on the big steel girders of the Empire State Building and although he nonetheless managed to possess a logical mind, facts sometimes rattled around in there and came spewing out at uninvited moments. But he had, or could get, the low down on everything, shady or legit, happening in Brooklyn. And right now I wanted to know a little more about this Collins guy before I showed up on his front doorstep.

"J.E. you say, huh, Harry?" he said as soon as my question had finished traveling the length of phone wire from Syd's store to his apartment. "Uh oh. Strictly Barracudasville there, pal. Uptown tough if you catch my drift."

"What does he do, Cudge. I mean uptown tough wise?" I straightened and played with the twisted wire as I sat in the closed-door-light-on booth.

"He? Ha! Harry. Everybody knows Janet Elizabeth's the daughter. Real man eater too. Best not take this one, Harold my friend. Can't win either way. Solve the case, the cops will think you're grandstanding, trying to make them look bad. Very harmful in the future cooperation department. Take it and don't solve it ... well, I wouldn't wanna be standin' in your shoes is all."

"You sound as if you already know what it's all about. Or am I too suspicious of your knowing ways?" I tugged the wire a little harder waiting for a straight answer.

"Ain't no secret. Her old man's been snatched. And in case you don't know, the old man's T.M. Collins. Mister Stock Market himself. You really should read a paper now and then, Harry. Improve the mind. Maybe even catch a case or two now and then." He was having fun and I played along.

"I been meaning to, Cudge, honest, but somebody keeps stealing Mrs. Geetus' Daily News before I can get to it."

"World's greatest detective." He laughed.

"You know who put the grab on?" I was serious.

"Harry. I'm surprised. Your old profession seems to come creeping back on you every now and then. You know I am a supplier of information and while that information, if used in the proper fashion, may lead you in a certain direction, I am not, by any stretch of the imagination, a stool pigeon." His tone of voice and proper phrasing said more than his words about how his feelings had been hurt and how I had been chastised at the same time.

"Sorry. Some habits are hard to break," I apologized, twisting the wire round my index finger.

"Yeah, especially the bad ones, I see," he accepted in full.

"Listen, I'll drop you a fin over at Farrell's tonight, or tomorrow at the latest."

"An honest man, Harry Parker. Not a bright one, 'cause I can tell from the sounds I'm getting that notwithstanding my advice you're going to take the case. But an honest one. Don't want to seem out of place here, Harry, but since you are going to get involved I'd appreciate the fin as soon as possible."

He hung up before I could respond. Not that there was much I could have said to that anyway. But I knew this Collins dame must be real trouble because it was one of the few times I had spoken to Cudge that he didn't come out with some obscure fact about the Empire State Building. The fall he had taken had seemed to trap trivial Empire State facts in his brain and they would come spilling out at just about any time. He would occasionally repeat some facts but it was amazing how much he knew about the building.

I let another nickel fill the slot and called the Collins place and told some hoarse sounding character who I was, and that I'd be there at seven-thirty. He said he would be sure to notify Miss Collins and dropped the receiver back into place before I could possibly contaminate his sensitive listening organ any further.

Skinny Vinny was very understanding and left me four dollars walking around money on my promise of twenty more as soon as I got my client's advance. In addition to fixing my radiator, he had tightened my side view mirror and topped off the tank while I was describing the cheating blonde and the Italian stud, "who, by the way," I had been cagey enough to throw in, "reminded me an awful lot of you." I avoided Doc's place figuring I probably wouldn't get shot again, at least not until after I got enough dough to pay him for the shoulder.

It was only five-thirty so I had some time to kill and nothing better to do than go back to my place and thumb my January issue of The National Geographic before grabbing a quick bite. After that I'd be driving over to see the "Barracuda." But for now I'd sink back with the Geographic. One of the few expenses I allowed myself to indulge in. I could forego the papers for months on end without the slightest remorse but I had been reading the National Geographic since I was a kid and looked forward to each issue like each new baseball season. I slid it out of its brown wrapper and once I'd passed the television and travel advertisements, I learned that Cuba filled America's sugar bowls. That this year alone Cuba would send more than 30 pounds of sugar for every man, woman and child in the country. America would be getting fat, I thought. Could we really be eating more than thirty pounds of sugar per person per year? It seemed impossible. Cuba had many more interesting facts that had certainly been kept secret from me. But my mind was elsewhere and for now reading my favorite magazine was going to be limited to glancing at the many pictures of Cuba, the Rhine, Canada's

Caribou Eskimos, the Adventures in Lololand, wherever the hell that was, and the Sponge Fisherman of Tarpon Springs.

I checked the Gold Medal Flour clock on the building down the street and realized I'd read past my meal time. Maybe, I thought, heading out the door on my way over to the Collins place, I'd decreased the per capita sugar intake by a gram or so.

CHAPTER 2

A butler was, of course, expected. But not one the size of Gargantua with the face of Mike Mazurki. I could tell right away that Cudge, as usual, had known more than he had given over.

"Mr. Parker, to see Miss Collins," I announced myself before any misunderstandings could arise.

"Wait there," he said and pointed to a spot I wanted to find exactly as he took my hat with one quick, strong motion that made me glad I had removed it from my head.

He disappeared into a labyrinth of doors that would have shamed any of those English hedge-row growers. And as I listened to the sounds of doors opening and closing and heels hitting marble growing fainter then louder, as he went and came back I noticed the ostentatiously high foyer ceiling dripping imported crystal chandeliers that hung, despite their wattage, like dark clouds about to rain on Harry Parker. I got a sudden flash of Cudge, snug in his apartment, smiling, listening to a comedy show on the radio, throwing back a Rheingold and reminiscing about the glory days, working on The Building.

"This way," the butler said, motioning in the same direction he had just traversed, "Miss Collins is in the Drawing Room."

"Oh, is she an artist?" I quipped.

"About as much as you're a comedian," he replied immediately, then closed the doors from the outside, as quiet as any second story man I'd ever known.

She was young. Almost younger than I'd remembered being and more beautiful than a Bensonhurst girl in the back seat of a Dodge. She was seated on the near end of a large white sofa, dressed in a white skirt and blouse with a man's style white double-breasted jacket. A black cat purred from her lap. Gargantua had already poured two cups of tea and put out a plate of cakes and pastries. He was so domestic. She hadn't bothered to wait for me; small crumbs from her white powdered bun fell onto the semi-catatonic cat curled in her lap. It didn't squirm, blink, or take any notice at all of the fact it was being littered on. It was one damn lazy cat.

She didn't say anything so I sat down and picked up the gooiest looking thing on the plate. I had not only missed dinner but I knew it would be quite some time before I had eats like these again. The thing had cream oozing out of every side after just one bite. She rang a little crystal bell and Gargantua returned as quickly as if he had been standing right outside the door the whole time. My bet was he had been.

"Mr. Parker requires a napkin, Charles," she said with all the clenched teeth politeness of fingernails being dragged across a blackboard, her gaze alternating between her bun and the cat but very definitely avoiding the oafish clod who sat opposite her. She had quite obviously been looking for a "nice" detective, one who wore a white shirt and tie and carried only a small, polite gun. What a disappointment I must be.

"No, Mr. Parker requires an explanation as to why he is here, Charles," I corrected, in an almost equally rude tone, while not taking my eyes from the very lovely Miss Collins.

"Mr. Parker is looking to get bounced on his ear." Charles had the final, only within my earshot, word on the subject as he handed me a linen napkin that was probably worth more than everything I was wearing, and maybe that brown sports jacket I'd never wear again thrown in. And I was now very deliberately rubbing custard all over it, and taking my time smearing it up real good, just in case Charles also pulled laundry duty around here.

"How does one get to be a detective, Mr. Parker?" J.E. asked, uninterested in my reply.

"Bad career choices." I sipped at my tea.

She gave a quick, half smile. "I see. Well, I'm afraid I never had the use for a private detective before, Mr. Parker, and I really don't know where to begin," she purred only slightly less lethargically than the old fuzzball in her lap.

"Well, suppose you just start at the beginning and keep going till the part where Charles here handed me the napkin. I'll be able to remember what happened from there. And, of course, don't leave out the part about your father being snatched. That's probably important."

She daintily plucked a cigarette from a fancy crystal dish on the coffee table and lit it with an even fancier looking gold and crystal lighter. She stared at the flame for a second or so before removing her thumb from the depressed button, extinguishing the flame. Then she breezed through a sad tale of the empty, lonely, rich, spoiled life she'd led and how tough it had been on her since the death of her mother when she was only twelve. How Daddy had immersed himself, totally, in his work, absorbed with the minutest of details, and left her to fend for herself with only a governess, a tutor and a few million bucks walking around money to comfort her.

Just about the time I was starting to reach for my hanky she took a small silver box from the table beside her. It was the kind expensive jewelry comes in. She looked at me for a long second, then opened it and tilted it so I could look inside. It was the famous opulent gold ring, with a setting of diminutive sparkling diamonds circling a perfectly centered ruby the size of an acorn that Mr. T. M. Collins always managed to hold aloft when a newspaper photographer or newsreel cameraman was on the scene. It was also still attached to a rather well manicured man's finger, if I was any judge of hairy knuckles. The finger was swaddled in dried blood-encrusted cotton, just laying there, betraying nothing of the pain which must have fairly recently run through it.

She was looking at me through cold blue eyes when I finally glanced up from Mr. Collins' digit. I thought that was kind of funny. Most dames, I figured, would either be looking right at that finger or looking away, either way in shock or repulsion. But she was carefully, unemotionally watching me for my reaction. Cool, calm, calculating. Just the way no man wants a dame to be. Unless of course he needs her to lie for him.

"Where's the note?" came my brash reaction.

"I have yet to receive a note." She sat quite erect and locked eyes with me when she spoke.

"Okay, then, when did you get the telephone call?"

"Mr. Parker, I have not, as of yet, been contacted." Her voice was a sharp, arrogant staccato.

I tried not to show my plebeian contempt, too much, but I guess it didn't work.

"Mr. Parker, 'Suspicion is the companion of mean souls, and the bane of all society,' Thomas Paine."

"'There is only one good, knowledge, and one evil, ignorance,' Socrates," I parried.

Her mouth opened, ever so slightly, and I felt about three feet taller than Gargantua and wished like hell I could still thank Sister Maria Beerkman for making me study one of the few things I had ever gotten to actually apply in real life. I'd give her a "Hail Mary" later.

"Call me if you decide you really want my services," I said as I started to get up.

"Harry. May I call you Harry?" Oh, she was foxy all right. Able to turn on the soft, sensual voice at a moment's notice.

"It's as good a name as any." I tried not to show the effect her baby-blues, not to mention her other more obvious ... charms, were having on me.

"Yes. Well, perhaps we've gotten off on bad footing here, Harry." She came this-close to sincerity.

"Yeah, if you mean perhaps I'm not the poor, hapless sap you thought I was when I first walked in the room, we did." That little heat of anger that forms red behind my ears was starting to thaw with the coolness of my reply.

"Mr. Mason to see you, ma'am," Charles interrupted, as a suave man of about my age, more well preserved and with much better looks walked in past him. His chin was square and jutting, his hair black, his skin tan and his gait to the manor born. His clothes were fresh from their wrappings and fit like they had been sculpted by Michelangelo. He was a man who could strut in place.

"Ah, here at last. Mr. Parker, Mr. Mason - my attorney." She said his name the way some people say Babe Ruth or Jack Dempsey. I failed to make the connection.

I got up and extended my hand and a broad smile. He read it well, probably from years of practice and said, "No. Before you even ask, it's John, not Perry." His voice was better than his looks and had a certain practiced ease about it that could only come from the Ivy League. It was blue-blood, aristocratic cultured and common man easy all at once.

"I hadn't even thought of the coincidence," I lied for no apparent reason.

She turned to him. "John, Mr. Parker is a private detective, I was just about to engage him as you came in."

"Really, Janet, I thought we agreed, no police." He gave me a haughty appraisal which I didn't like one bit and then added a bit too eruditely, "Of any kind."

"No, John, you agreed. I said that I would consider it. And I have. Now I have engaged Mr. Parker."

"Now, Janet, I didn't mean to impose my will, but let's not be unreasonable." He gave me that look-down-his-nose glance again but before he could add any further insults, I interrupted.

"Let's get one thing straight, lady, nobody's 'engaged' no-body yet. It ain't that easy, I have to agree to get engaged first. Then there's the how-much-a-day plus expenses courtship period. Followed by the you start telling me the truth, the whole truth and nothing but the truth get to know each other better, light petting process. Then, and only then, do we shop for a ring. Maybe."

I took a long look of my own, at the advancing form of Charles Gargantua Mazurki, noted that there was no elephant gun within arm's reach, and added, as I rose, "Unless of course this is a shot-gun engagement."

Miss Collins was the only one who seemed even slightly amused by my remark. She waved her magic hand in a very blase manner and Gargantua stopped about a foot or so short of where I was standing by the sofa, and picked up the empty tea cup as if it was what he had been stalking all along.

John "Perry" Mason sat in the over-stuffed, over-decorated chair nearest the fireplace like a schoolboy who had just given the wrong answer and had been admonished in front of the entire class·by the teacher he had a crush on. He leaned nervously forward, head never touching the fine lace antimacassars on the winged back of the chair.

The Collins Barracuda and Harry Parker were the only ones left standing and I was feeling pretty damn good about myself when it suddenly hit me that Cudge hadn't given me any Empire State Building facts because he, head beater of some very tough heads, was afraid of this woman I now stood with face to face. I sank back down into the sofa opposite Charles and wondered what duties, beside butlering, he performed for the Collins clan.

"Perry" must have decided I was as wiped as he was because he gave me one of his best smug looks and said, "Detectives? I thought they inhabited cheap hotel lobbies and had eyes in the shape of keyholes."

"No," I said, "that's dirty divorce or sleazy tax-shelter lawyers. By the way, what exactly is it you do for Miss Collins? She's not up for murder or anything is she?"

"Oh really, Janet, this is preposterous," he intoned. "How can you trust your father's life to a man with the sensitivities of a common gusseteer?"

He spoke in elegant, polished phrases. And I was going to be sure to look this one up.

"Boys, please. I would prefer that we all work together on this." The society hostess charm oozed out on every word she spoke so her sentence was one liquid flowing plea for peace and harmony among all God's creatures.

I wasn't sure of much at this point but I was sure I didn't want to work on this, together, or otherwise, despite her winning ways. The whole thing stunk. A wealthy and powerful dame calling me in to rescue her even richer and more powerful father. Where did she even get my name? Why did she have a butler as big, strong and ugly as a Pittsburgh steel worker? And most of all I despised and distrusted John "Perry" Mason. He was old money with old "keep the poor man down" attitudes. The kind that had probably worked my old man to death in those factories all his life without the decency to even notice he'd existed. I certainly didn't want to be looking at his rich, smug mug for any extended period of time.

This time I was really going to leave. I shifted in my seat and that's when I made my fatal mistake. I took one more gander at Mr. Collins' lonely rubied finger. Some of the cotton had shifted when she had placed the box on the table and I noticed my first impression had been way off. Whoever did the chopping, and chopped it was because it was too mangled to have been cut, had gone to a lot of trouble not only to inflict pain on Mr. Collins, but to make sure to leave the thing such a mess that Miss Collins would know exactly what her father had gone through.

"Mr. Parker," she said, catching my weight shift or reading my mind. "I can pay you a great deal of money, quite a bit more than your standard fee, I assure you. Won't you reconsider and help me?"

I had to admit, for a rich, powerful dame, she played the poor, helpless woman angle to perfection.

"Well, just what are you worth, Miss Collins?" I knew from a few well placed telephone calls about what she could cough up in an emergency but I sometimes like to gauge people, especially ones playing the helpless women angle, by their reactions to my impertinent questions.

"Tacky, tacky, Mr. Parker. Such questions are not asked in polite circles."

"That's okay. You can call me tacky. Some people I know tell me I'm downright rude. Same people say your net worth is somewhere around fifty million bucks."

She lit another cigarette, and let that ornate gold and crystal lighter slide across the oversized coffee table in the general direction of the opulent crystal ashtray. She wore the overall appearance of one who was truly bored with such monetarily mundane questions. "I would say that that's in the approximate neighborhood," she let out with a puff of smoke.

"Fifty million, that's a nice neighborhood, Miss Collins. Don't imagine you'd have to take in boarders."

"Mr. Parker, you haven't answered my question as to whether or not you would take my case. Say a four hundred dollar retainer and a hundred a day, plus expenses."

A bunch of questions rushed through my mind. The biggest of which of course was, why me? But they were all out-weighed by my now down to four bucks bank roll and my forty-three dollar, due next Wednesday, rent.

I decided that Cudge could answer most of my questions so I figured the little guy, from the wrong side of whatever was the present-day dividing line of town, might as well throw this little party a curve.

"First, answer a question for me," I said throwing a Camel in my mouth and torching it with my reliable, plain looking Zippo lighter.

"If I can," she said as if she knew there was no question that I could possibly ask that she could not answer.

"I know your father's T.M. Collins, richest man since the Crash. Kept all his money by getting out just in time. Then getting back in with the same shrewd business savvy. But what in God's name is the matter with you people?"

"What on earth do you mean, Mr. Parker?" She seemed genuinely puzzled.

"I mean J.E., T.M. the richest people in town and you can't seem to afford whole names. I know your moniker, what's the T.M. short for?"

"Nothing. Father just decided to take an O out of his name."

"Just decided. Who just decides to take an O out of their name?"

"I would guess, Mr. Parker, that you have never tried going through life being called Tom Collins."

"Well, J.E., you've got me there."

"Well, as long as I've got you, let me ask you a question, Mr. Parker."

"Shoot."

"What's your first move?" She was rather forcefully extinguishing her cigarette in the ashtray and appearing to be giving it her full attention as she waited to hear what I had in mind.

I picked up the little silver box and gave it a good size shake. She looked at the box, then at me. "Goin' to take this to a friend of mine down at the lab," I said, catching the ruby's red glint in the light of the floor lamp behind me.

"Janet! I insist, no police." Mason was as firm as I guessed he was ever going to get with her. She let her eyes slide from his to mine.

"Listen, Mason, that's the second time you said, 'no police,' don't you know this thing's been in every paper in town already? How do you intend to keep the police out of it?"

"Suppose you allow me to worry about that aspect of the case, and you just try to concentrate on keeping them out of it on your end."

I turned back to J.E. whose eyes seemed to be waiting there for me and said, "I said he was a friend, there'll be no cops in on it, I assure you."

"What are you going to have your friend at the lab do?" she inquired with as casual an interest as one might pay a leaf floating down from a tree.

"I just want to be as sure as you are of what we're dealing with here is all. I'm going to check this fingerprint."

"Oh my God, Janet," Mason bellowed, slapping his hand to his forehead in absolute horror, "how morbid can this cretin get?" He was on his feet and closing in on Janet, probably a court room tactic along the lines that a closer appeal will be heard more favorably.

"Be still, John. I'd have doubted Mr. Parker's abilities if that were not to be his first move." Her smile was full and warm and her head shook in a slight affirmative motion.

The Barracuda was a cool one all right.

CHAPTER 3

TUESDAY, JANUARY 7TH

The room had that familiar spin going as I pulled open the top drawer of the nightstand and reached in for my eye opener. It had been a long night. I had left the pleasant trio on Pierrepont Street and had gone over to meet Cudge at Farrell's, a local watering hole that had quenched many a Brooklyn desert thirst. He had appreciated the fin and the beers I bought him using some of the money from my four-hundred dollar retainer. I had gotten there late having stopped off first at Vinny's and slipped the twenty and a note through his mail slot, which he also used for people returning keys to cars they had rented from him for the night. It was a good set up, keeping each customers car an extra day or two after it was fixed and running a rental business on the side. I wondered how many times over the years my old Buick had been rented to some pimply faced kid out on a first date and secretly hoped it hadn't seen too much more action than I had. Then I had shot on over to Smith Street and seen Doc Dearborn and chewed him down to a reasonable rate with a reminder of the sweet young "nurse" I had surgically removed from his very married back. I had some bucks and could have easily paid him more, but it never hurts to work on your chewing-down routine. Besides I didn't want to set any new bullet removal price standards that I would have to live up to in the Collins-less future.

A few drafts served by Joe, the lady killer bartender, in that round cardboard container could do more to loosen Cudge's tongue than anything the Japs or Nazis had ever thought up. He had been in the war, they were desperate times and even men who had fallen from buildings had been drafted. Although, one-eyed cops with bad backs had not. Cudge had even been a prisoner in a Stalag. I smiled thinking of the amazement on some Goosestepper's face after having asked Cudge about gun emplacements and getting a "Did you know that there are 1,860 steps to the top of the Empire State Building?" thrown back at him in rapid fire reply. It would be really funny, I thought to have been able to hear their long line of questions being answered in window, steps, elevator amounts, read off by Cudge in a Name, Rank, Serial Number litany of unintended smoke screen bombardment.

The shot was beginning to work as another one of those mornings-after began to fade into normal day. My head was starting to clear, well, at least enough to remember some more of last night's conversation. Cudge had told me that Mr. John Mason was an extremely influential man with the extremely influential set. A Doctor of Jurisprudence, full partner in a major law firm exceedingly convincing with juries, commanding extravagant legal fees and a man who makes exceptionally wise investments. He had begun his career with the District Attorney's Office but had made a sudden and very successful switch to defense attorney with the infamous Biddenger case. Biddenger was an oil man who through no coincidence went from millions to hundreds of millions during the war years. Then came allegations, and finally charges of treason, selling oil to both the Germans and the Italians. Mason had left the D.A.'s office on a Friday afternoon and was working for

Biddenger the following Monday morning. Swearing, no conflict of interest, all the way to the bank.

Biddenger was as guilty as Hitler and Mussolini, but Mason was as tactically overbearing as Patton. After a brief trial Biddenger walked, and Mason has been a wealthy man with an outstanding clientele ever since.

He was said to be decidedly interested in Miss Collins. She showed a moderate interest in return. Or as much interest as she had shown in anything, other than Daddy's money. Rumor has it she was more frigid than my old Coldspot, Cudge went on, and I suddenly found myself thinking of guys down on the docks talking of cold women in terms of Harry Parker's refrigerator and couldn't help but wonder whose appliance they measured the hot ones by. Joe came to mind about the same time as thoughts of hot women. The big drawback in the whole J.E. and Mason getting together thing seemed to be T.M.'s objections to the age difference. Cudge thought this was rather ironic since T.M. was spending more and more time in Joe's Place and he wasn't spending his time chatting with Joe either, if I knew what he meant. I said I did and he said, sure you do. He said T.M. spends his time with a woman named Ruby, he must have something for the gemstone, and she was the kind of woman who would do just about anything for money if you know what I'm saying here. I said I caught what he was throwing, and he asked if he had ever told me how many steps there are to the top of the Empire State Building. Like a sap I said no and that's when I heard all about his German interrogators, their penchant for twisting certain appendages of the human body in directions not normally meant to twist and their total lack of appreciation for the artistic splendor of the Great Building.

It took me about three more beers and a half an hour to lead him back around to the Collins clan and find out that despite the word on the street he really thought T.M. wasn't so much opposed to Mason's age as he was to his business practices. Somewhere along the line he had also managed to slip in, very matter of factly, that good old Charles had done a stretch, for manslaughter, in "the Castle on the Hudson," Brooklynese for Sing Sing. He had killed the wife of his former employer with an axe. "Because he asked me to," he had calmly explained at his trial. I made a mental note to treat Charles with a little more respect and wondered about what size axe it took to chop off a ring finger.

Enough remembering, for now, I thought, as I shoved my feet into those god-damned Thelma-given slippers and shuffled over to the hot plate to heat up some of yesterday's Maxwell House, which was yet another provision getting down to the last drop. I sat in my usual chair and waited for the perk. I took a quick gander, but there was no mail in the chair by the door.

Cudge had promised, for an extra fin, to get to work on the gnawing question to which he hadn't had an answer. Why me?

Where did the Collins dame get my name and why didn't she use one of the Big Boys with the Big Reps? Detectives who had actually worked on kidnapping cases in the past and maybe even knew how the hell one goes about finding kidnappers who as a rule are not the most patient of people. Not to sell myself entirely short, I was a damned good cop in my day, although, since going private most of my cases involved cameras in bushes, I had actually solved two murders.

But kidnapping's a different story. It's kind of a half preventive crime. Stumbling around in the dark until you put the grab on the mug that did it, my usual modus operandi, just doesn't cut it on a snatch job. You've got to catch on quick enough to stop the worst part from happening. You can't have your client taken for the ransom money and wind up with a dead loved one and expect to stay in business all that long. Frankly, I wasn't so sure that Mason's discerning eye appraisal of me wasn't right, that maybe too many peeper jobs had come between me and good detective work. Maybe these circumstances were not the most conducive under which to attempt to re-hone my old deductive skills.

I poured the java and waited for the radio to warm up. It didn't take it too long to get hot. The first story out of the box was about T.M.'s "disappearance" with the reporter taking great pleasure in adding " ... and when questioned, Captain James Quiggly of the downtown Brooklyn Division said he had seen the reports in the papers and had tried to contact Miss Collins regarding the matter and had been informed by her attorney, John Mason, that she was out of town and could not be reached for a few days."

Oh, what a piece of work you are Perry, you pompous, self-righteous son of a bitch you.

Quiggly was a damned good man. Tough but fair, as they say. I had known him back in the good old pre-Kaminsky days. He had been my sergeant for a short time in the 83rd precinct down on Wilson and DeKalb, a brick fortress of a building complete with turrets. He was smart with the books and with the street and rose very quickly through the ranks. I could imagine how stupid he was feeling talking to that reporter and saying he "had tried to contact Miss Collins regarding the matter but. ... " Quiggly was a good cop and must have known for sure that Collins was sitting comfortably up in her Pierrepont Street home as sure as he was sweating bullets down in his precinct. Quiggly had moved his division into the top floor of the 83rd. Maybe out of nostalgia, or maybe to keep a better eye on Kaminsky, but more than likely for its proximity to the area in Brooklyn where most of his work came from.

The java was finished and so were my trivial reminiscences so I got dressed and headed over to see Doc Cutter. Nobody knew for sure whether he was a real doctor or not. He worked in the police lab located in the basement of the 83rd and everybody called him Doc and that was fine by me. For a little pleasant conversation and common respect he would get to your report first and keep the secret of the ages to boot.

I got to the lab about seven a.m. Long before the regular cops would show up yet well after Cutter had arrived. I had learned to get to him early years before and it had always paid off.

"Hey, Harry, how the heck are ya." He barely looked up from whatever it was he had trapped between two slides under his microscope.

"Hey, Doc," I answered. He looked his usual - dressed- right-out-of-the-clothes-hamper-self. White lab coat trailing on his short frame, almost touching the floor, smeared with every kind of stain, animal, vegetable, mineral and unimaginable. Remnants from every case he'd worked on and probably about half the lunches he'd eaten in the past six years. It was definitely not the same coat he was wearing the morning Frankie Palms had broken in to steal some evidence from his boss' case and drilled Doc in the gut when the brave little bastard had refused to give it up. Frankie Palms, if I remembered correctly, had earned his moniker from his proclivity for spending long periods of time in the bathroom with magazines of the certain undraped women variety. I believe he had a particular penchant for beach volleyball.

I had walked in on this small scale massacre and had subsequently ended Frankie's rather unbrilliant criminal career by putting too much lead in his diet. And in that way had also helped convict Louie Laronissi of murder one. I had also saved Doc's life by getting him over to Brooklyn Hospital in my car rather than waiting for an ambulance.

Doc's about five foot nothing and weighs about one-oh-five and if I were ten foot tall instead of six-two he'd be the half my size he sometimes seems. He has bushy hair that looks like it has never been introduced to a comb and Coke bottle wire-rimmed eyeglasses that seem forever to be just-this-close to slipping off the bridge of his nose. He is that rare combination of willy-nilly-bull-dog who always gets the job done and never gripes about what's been given him.

If he knew I had been bounced from the force he never mentioned it. And over the past few years he's kept working on my cases as if I were still one of the boys.

"Whattya got for me, Harry?" His voice was its usual friendly tone.

"Just a print job, Doc, easy one too," I jawed lightly.

"Did you lift it clean?" he asked while inertly studying his microscopic specimen.

"Don't want to brag, but it's lifted better than if you had done the job yourself."

He peeked over the top of his glasses and smiled in disbelief, but said nothing.

I took the little silver box from my pocket and opened it. He didn't even blink. He just nodded, took the finger out, pressed it on his ink pad and then rolled it onto an index file card, wiped the finger on his lab coat and stuck it back in the box.

"Real smooth job, Harry. Remind me, if I ever get married, to have you get my mother-in-law's prints for me."

"Sure thing, only do yourself a favor and skip the altar scene." I slipped my hat back on and pulled the brim down.

"Have it for you tonight," he said.

"I'm already pretty sure whose it is," I said.

"Now, Harry, that would be cheating." He peered at me over his glasses again. This time it was school teacher admonishment that looked at me, and the look was not accompanied by a smile.

"He's not a criminal," I blurted, but stopped short of telling him who I was all but positive it was.

"Harry, please. Give me a chance to show off my skills." His professional pride raised the pitch of his voice an octave or two.

"Okay. I'll see you tonight then," I said as I walked out. "You can catch me at Farrell's any time after ten or so. Give me what you get if I'm still standin', if not, slip a note in my pocket."

"I'll be sure to bring some paper and a pen," he said turning his attention back to the slide under his microscope, giving a low "Uh - Ah," and writing something in his handy note book.

"Hey, Harry," he said, stopping me short of the steps. "I may be a little late, just remembered the car's on the fritz, it's in the shop."

I slid my keys along the top of his workbench. "Take it easy on the old girl, Doc, she's just back from Vinny's herself."

"How are you going to get around?"

"Got it covered, only a few places to get to today anyway and you can give me the keys back when you catch up with me at Farrell's." I took the steps two at a time, feeling younger than I had in a while, at least until I was about halfway up anyway.

CHAPTER 4

I took the train to Court Street and remembered why I had always thought the subway was aptly named -- the bare-bulbed
unilluminated sordidness of the place, even in midmorning, gray
was as good as it got. Funny too, because when you think about
it you realize that the subway was built at a time when things were
still being done in a grand scale in the city. Yet outside of different
small mosaics, white tile and cement seems to have been the great
scheme for almost every station. Court Street was even in the best
part of town. The same stop I would have gotten off to go to the
Collins place on Pierrepont if Vinny hadn't come through on the
radiator and it was just like all the others. I got off here because I
wanted a good long walk back to my hovel. Get some much needed exercise and take in the atmosphere of the very extravagant
houses of "the other half." That's the beauty of Brooklyn, a twenty
or thirty minute walk can be all it takes to separate the haves from
the have nots. The extra money in my pocket must have made me
a little giddy because walking along Court Street I stopped for a
cup of coffee and bought a newspaper. Having money can be a
dangerous thing. Before hitting home, I stopped off at old man
Whelan's grocery, paid my back tab and bought enough provisions

to make the old Coldspot look halfway presentable should anyone but me ever see the inside of it. Even stopped in at Greenstein's drugstore for a pack of Blue Star double edge razor blades and some Ben-Gay for my aching shoulder.

The Brooklyn Eagle, which was starting to become a real news-paper, with actual hard hitting stories, rather than a social regis-ter for the downtown crowd, carried the best picture of T.M. A bust shot of great facial clarity, nevertheless managing to show that its subject was wearing a tuxedo. To the untrained eye his hand would seem to have been caught adjusting his tie just as the camera clicked, but to those who knew, it was his way of getting The Ring in the picture. The paper wasn't about to completely abandon its prim and proper past overnight. T.M.'s picture and the story of his disappearance ran alongside a small article which promised an investigation into allegations of far reaching police corruption. Yeah, well what year hadn't some newspaper publisher hell bent on reform promised that, I thought.

Anyway, I now had a good picture of T.M. to show around if I needed it. I ripped it out of the paper and folded it into my wallet. Mrs. Geetus came into the room and dropped an envelope onto the chair. She saw me at the table.

"Just getting up?" She managed to sound almost tolerant of my deviant behavior.

"I'm on a case." I found it was always easier to just go along with her.

"No shooting in here, like on that last one. On this I am stead-fast, Mr. Parker."

She was referring to a case I had about a year ago, the one where I had so brilliantly put the chair under the doorknob for protection. A couple of bad shooters had missed me by a country mile from the roof of a house across the street. But they had left four bullet holes in Mrs. Geetus' precious walls. Mrs. Geetus had fixed the walls by covering the holes with three of the worst pictures ever painted and raising my rent three dollars a month. I made sure to keep the pictures in place, hoping she'd forget the holes and not make the three dollar raising of rent a yearly ritual. She brought the shooting incident up whenever she heard I was on a case, or whenever some unknown urge struck her.

"No shooting, I promise." I handed her this and next month's rent and she left with a big smile, forgetting all about guns, holes in walls, and my late waking habits and just about everything else except the location of her passbook and the directions to her bank.

I decided to use the newly gained peace to get back to the Geographic. The first "Natural Color Photograph" was of Cuba's National Capitol Building, which was 308 feet high. Not exactly an Empire State Building, I mused. But I was much more interested in the two ladies walking in the foreground. Skirts short, heels high, and legs turned in all the right angles. I was alert enough to notice that the same pretty young señorita adorned both the black and white photo on page 30 and the color one on page 47, although the negative had been reversed on one of them because the buttons on her dress were on different sides.

It may be time to call one of my women friends for a date.

The photo on page 58, of the badly bombed Frankfurt Railway station was taken at 1:15, unless the big hanging clock was part of the area the bombing had laid claim to. There was no way of tell-ing if the 1:15 was an a.m. or a p.m.

A model showed much of herself and very little of the new German fashion materials in a picture I certainly hoped was of things soon to come.

Nothing much caught my eye with the Caribou Eskimos or in Lololand, which by the way is in southwest China. I didn't exactly soak up much from the Sponge Fisherman of Tarpon Springs ei-ther and by the time I got to the back cover sporting a Hormel whole Chicken advertisement I realized that I had once again gone through my monthly fill of the Geographic in about a day. I prom-ised myself each month it wouldn't happen this time, but each time I lied to myself again.

In any event it was too early to head to Farrell's so I decided to see what was in the envelope Mrs. Geetus had dropped off. I guess embossed envelopes with no stamps are the only kind Miss Collins deals in because I could feel that left-hand corner sticking out as soon as I picked it up.

What progress have you made

That was it. A whole piece of paper, an envelope and another delivery man used up on five lousy words. Not even a Dear Mr. Parker, or a Truly yours. Hell, she had even left off the question mark, although my guess was this was phrased to be more of a command than a question.

I took a few nickels from Suzy, the porcelain cookie jar shaped like a cat that sits on the table almost as catatonically as Miss Collins' cat sits on her lap. It always made me feel strange, taking her head off just to get a cookie or a Twinkie but somehow it was okay going in there for more important things, like nickels or unpaid bills or a bullet or two for my .45. I was going down to Syd's to give Miss Collins a call and to tell her not to expect up to the minute reports. It hadn't even been a full twenty-four hours since I left her. On the way I decided to take her note and slip it under Mr. Bellem's door. It seemed a much more intriguing question to pose to a man who was seeing another man's wife and it seemed a small, 'though childish payback to those early morning wake up honks.

I braced myself, collar turned up, hat pulled down, as the wind seemed to whip from every direction and I was glad Syd's was only around the block from my Union Street abode. Both telephone booths were occupied when I got there. The one on the left had a girl of about high school age with a row of nickels lined up on the little counter under the phone that told me she was having boyfriend trouble and might have to be dragged out of there come closing time. The booth on the right, my booth, had an older, screwy looking dame in a Hedda Hopper happy hat that almost had me laughing in her face. At least she had no nickels lined up. I tapped on the glass, pointed to my watch and gave her that universal, "how much longer are you going to be" gesticulation. She turned toward the wall and through the door I could hear her say, "Harold, there's the strangest looking man outside the booth, I think he intends to molest me. Call the police."

I could tell that informing her that she was perfectly safe, that I had no intention, in her dreams, or otherwise, of molesting her, or that she was in my booth would do me no good. And knowing how long it would take the police to react to Harold's call and that she wasn't about to come out until they showed. Or I left and remembering that stack of nickels on the other girl's counter, I decided it was time to catch up on some old times with Syd. Maybe I'd even have a Coke while I was at it. Syd was probably only a couple of years older than me, but with his bald head, gray hair at the sides, and his short, squat body, he looked to be somewhere in his mid to late fifties, maybe more. He was now, as usual, yelling at the kids at the other side of the store to keep their hands off the merchandise. The racks with the candy, comic books, toy whistles and other assorted kiddy merchandise were stacked all together, opposite the phone booths and were forbidden treasures to those without money. Syd spent most of his time down that end of the counter, "Watching for the trouble makers, who'd rob your eyes if you turned your head." Which, if you thought about it showed great speed and dexterity on their part.

He treated candy like gold, at least until someone else had paid for it, then like all good businessmen he could care less about what happened to it.

"Maybe we should put a sign up on that booth on the right, Syd," I said as I took a stool at the counter. "How does 'Harry Parker's Office' sound?"

"How does an extra two dollars a month sound?"

"It was just a thought," I said. "I'll wait for one of them to leave. I think I'll go back to my office and give the dame in my booth some room to retreat. Give me a call when she goes, will ya?" I decided on a glass of water instead of the Coke and as Syd poured he gave a glance at the booth and nodded his head in agreement. I slipped on back past the Life Savers and Wise Potato Chip bags that were the latest items to take up most of the space of the tiny hallway that led back to my office.

My ever decreasing share of the storeroom consisted of a small wooden desk with a chair on either side of it and one very dirty, very large window behind it. There was a coat rack in the corner, but it had been a long time since it could support anything more than a light sweater. I put my hat and coat on top of whatever box currently took up the space closest to the desk. Clients, for some reason, usually preferred to keep theirs on.

My daily ritual was to turn my chair around and slide it slightly away from the desk, tilt it on its back two legs, lean it against the desk and stare at the brown hazy window, waiting for myopic parts of cases to come clearly into focus. Sometimes, I found, if I stared long and hard enough, I would hit just the right reflective angle and the stains on the window would take on the shapes of the faces of the people or of the places of whatever case I was currently working on. Sometimes, I'd just get a stiff neck.

I was in this position when a soft, unexpected, "Harry" came from behind me.

I almost fell over trying to turn around too fast.

"Well, what are you doing in this part of town, J.E., looking for some Halvah?"

"Some what?" she said with obvious ignorance of the candy of the masses.

"Never mind, just a little joke. I take it you want to see me?" I also took it that I'd have to remind Syd about telling me when people were there to see me and not just sending them back. Some people who come to see me aren't as friendly as others.

"You didn't answer my note" My God, I thought, she's taken to delivering the notes verbally. They're still five worders and they still sound way too demanding, but the package they were delivered in beat the hell out of any envelope ever made.

"Money doesn't buy everything after all, Miss Collins. I don't answer notes, or have a delivery boy, or run when the mistress whistles. And I don't dash to a phone because you happen to have an urge for an update. That's not what your four hundred gets you."

"What does it get me, Mr. Parker?" The edge on her voice was sharper than my new Blue Star blade and I had a feeling she could serve up a real close shave.

"It gets you results, not book reports. If that's not to your liking, ya found ya way in, I'd bet you can find it back out again. Only don't go askin' for no refunds, 'cause my firm policy is to retain retainers."

"Have you found out anything at all yet?" Her tone had climbed down off the cutting edge however it was still too sharp to be considered anything approaching civility.

"A couple of things."

"Like?"

"Like your father hangs out with a real money grabber, named Ruby. Like Perry Mason's in love, or lust, or both with you. And that Germans don't particularly like the Empire State Building."

"I could have told you the first two last night," she said without the least trace of interest or surprise in the third.

"Then you should have, Miss Collins. You could have saved me a night's work and yourself one hell of a bar tab."

She gave me a quizzical look.

"You did say, plus expenses, remember?"

"Your getting drunk is not expenses!"

"No, but my getting others drunk enough to talk is." The hell my getting drunk wasn't part of expenses. It would probably wind up being the biggest part, especially if these damn notes kept coming.

"And what are you going to do now?"

"Now, I'm going to turn my chair back around, wait for you to go wherever it is you go, and continue thinking. And then tonight I'm going to meet a guy who has promised to deliver some information, for a nominal fee, of course."

"Do try to get a little more information and a little less bar tab, Mr. Parker."

"I'll do what it takes, J.E. Nothing more you'd care to tell me is there? Help me on my way to hunting up a fact or two that perhaps you're not already aware of. Might be able to save some time that way, not to mention alcoholic expenses."

"No, I don't believe so. Now that you know all about Ruby, John and the German situation I believe you're pretty much up on everything. Do however be good enough to notify me if you penetrate the identity of my father's captors." The words literally snapped out of her mouth with the same delivery I imagined one uses on new servants who perhaps don't yet know their places. She spun on her heels and only her beauty saved her from the comic sight of a few hundred dollars worth of Mr. Somebody's designer frock squeezing between columns of potato chip cartons and Milky Way boxes.

Syd came in and announced, "The Hat Lady has left the booth," with vigilance in his voice.

"And the person I was going to call has left the store," I only slightly deflated his pride.

He raised an eyebrow and looked at the departing Miss Collins then walked back through the ever narrowing passageway. I just didn't think the time was right to bring up the dangers of letting people walk in unannounced while he was following a dream.

I waited around a while, looking at the window and thinking things over, before I took the train back to Farrell's.

CHAPTER 5

C udge was still drawing a blank on how Miss Collins had drawn my name from the vast, unaccomplished pool of second rate dicks, although he did phrase it quite less critically. "Somebody buried this information very deep," he said, his eyes going down, not wanting to meet mine, "very deep," he repeated a little lower. He did give me the address where I could find Ruby though and added the good news that Doc had dropped my car off while out on a call. A prowl car had followed him out and taken him back from here. Then Cudge threw in that there are six thousand five hundred windows in the Empire State Building. I was glad to see he was overcoming his fear of J.E. Collins. And, I suppose, one can never know too much about the Empire State Building.

I dropped Cudge a fin, pried Joe away from his "latest," paid for the beers and headed for the old Buick. I drove a couple of miles to some hole in the wall that you had to walk down four steps to get into, over on Sterling Place. The sign said "Joe's," the bartender's name was Phil, and he said the place was owned by a gal named Ruby. It had all the makings of an interesting evening. What kind of mom names a tiny, wrinkly, new born cuddly kid Ruby, I thought, then remembered a childhood friend named Libby Lipschitz and withdrew my own rhetorical question.

"How's business tonight?" I asked Phil in the most engaging tone I could muster.

"Usual." He seemed barely able to squeeze the breath past his tight little lips.

"Not being from around here, what's usual?" I pumped.

"'Bout what you see," Phil, the multisyllabic, gestured around the very empty bar.

I smiled. Phil sort of snorted back. He wore a very "I'm retired from something else, I'm just doing this for a couple of bucks, and I ain't tellin' you nothin'" look on his mug that I didn't like just enough to want to rearrange.

The joint was dark and musty and less promising than a nunnery.

"Looking for me?"

A smooth, slow breath of desert heat crept across the nape of my neck and shifted the hang of my shorts noticeably to the foreground.

I turned slowly, more from anxious anticipation than from inquisitiveness. She filled the doorway like a cork stopper in a champagne bottle and I had a feeling she was due for one very loud pop. I smiled as best as I could and searched for what seemed like forever for the muscles that made my mouth move. If I wasn't looking for her I was certainly prepared to lie about it.

"Ruby? The owner of this ... establishment?" The seventh facial nerve kicked into gear after an eternity of banal smile.

"Right on both counts. Care to parlay that bet, honey, or are you satisfied with what you got?"

She was a knockout. Long red hair flowed over her bare shoulders. A red dress that began just above where I imagined her nipples to be poured over the rest of her body like a liquid sunset. Oh there was no doubt with Ruby you knew just what you were getting. Hopefully.

"I'm Harry Parker, working on the Collins case. I suppose you've heard old T.M.'s gone missing? I'd like to ask you a few questions, if you don't mind?" I took a long drag on my butt and made sure to exhale in Phil's direction. I didn't think I'd get too upset if he took offense.

She motioned me to a table in the rear left corner of the joint and I drank her in like a dying man in a desert as she led the way. I showed I'd been brought up right sitting only after she had. Phil appeared with two bourbons, neat. And disappeared with the same Shadow-like ability. Did he know what evil lurked in the hearts of men? If he did, it'd be a damn good bet you'd never get it out of him.

"You're too polite to be a cop, Harry. Private dick?" She pronounced the last two words like an invitation.

"Let's just say I've been hired to find out certain things and chief among them is why one of the richest men in New York would frequent ... well, why he spent as much time here as he did. Although, now that I've seen you. ..."

"Slow down a minute. Don't go making one and one add up to three just yet, Mr. Detective. I know Collins, yes. And he used to come in here a lot, but he stopped comin' in about a week ago and he didn't come here to see me."

"You've got to be kidding. I mean no offense, but take a good look around, you are the scenery."

"Thank you." She smiled, took a healthy dose of bourbon and leaned back in her seat. "Just the same he always brought his own scenery with him. Big blonde, built like the brickyard worked double shifts for a month of Sunday's just to fill her order."

I gave her my best, head-cock-to-the-right, "come on, lady" look. It was usually good enough to send a person back to the drawing board for a second attempt at truth or reason, or just a better lie.

"Okay, don't believe me. Go ask Phil there. I'll wait right here so you don't think I'm slipping him any signals or anything."

"I somehow don't seem to be able to get much out of old Yes sir, no sir, have you any dough sir, Phil," I said.

Now she laughed. It was a good, low, pretty voiced laugh that kissed my cheek and lightened the mood of the dingy joint.

"You've got him down pretty good," she said, "but he'll talk to you now. Now that he's seen I have."

I didn't expect much but I took a slow walk on over to the bar just the same. "Hi, Phil. Ruby there says you feel like talkin' now, that so?"

"What's on your mind?" His mood had done a one-eighty, his lips had actually parted, although, they were still very far from full.

I reached for my wallet, took out the picture of Collins and shoved it across the bar. "Ever see this guy in here?"

"Plenty." He was leaning across the bar, swirling a towel around inside a glass. It wasn't going to get any cleaner or dryer.

"Was he alone?"

"Are you kidding? Blonde, about half his age. Give your right nut for one night in the sack with her."

"When's the last time you saw them in here."

"'Bout four, five nights ago." I was beginning to wonder if friction could break a glass.

"About how long had they been comin' in?"

"I don't know. Maybe a month. Maybe more." If the glass in his hand had been allowed to stop twirling long enough to reflect his emotion it wouldn't have bothered.

"Ever hear any of what they talked about?" I pressed on.

"Naw. Always took the corner booth, back where Ruby is now. Ordered champagne by the bottle. Stayed to themselves. You ever run out of questions?"

"Just one more."

"Yeah, what's that?"

"You wouldn't lie to me, would you Phil?"

Phil just smiled, finally put the glass on top of a pyramid of glasses he had built with all his spare time and went back to wiping down the bar. He was a very clean guy. I walked over to Ruby, thanked her for her cooperation and said goodnight.

"Get what you were after, honey?" She laughed loud and hard.

"You'll know when I do," I said not knowing what the hell I meant, but it cut her laugh off like a slug to the heart and I widened my smile to show I knew something, that I didn't.

I sat in the Buick for a while before starting the motor. I was wondering how long it took those two to work up the blonde story and how much rehearsal time they had before I had finally gotten around to them. Cudge had never steered me wrong yet and I was willing to bet that if he said T.M. was seeing Ruby then Ruby was who he was seeing and not some blonde bimbo who had brickyards working overtime filling out her form, intriguing as it may be to find her.

It was a good story though and they played their roles to perfection, I'll give them that. Something besides the made up blonde was bothering me but I couldn't finger it. I pulled the Buick to the corner and playing a hunch decided to tail the first one of them that came out. Not much of a plan really, but sometimes it's the spur of the moment choices that pan out. In real life it doesn't just come to you like it does in the Ellery Queen books.

I threw another butt out the window onto the asphalt ashtray and checked my watch for how many seconds had passed since I had last looked. Twenty-three, more or less. Waiting always made me edgy. I never heard a sound. Just felt the cold steel pressed against my neck as I sat there watching Joe's.

"Sliding in behind ya, bub. Don't say a word, just drive straight to your joint, we'll do our talkin' there. Obey the traffic rules and try not to pass any cops along the way and maybe you'll get out of this with your head still where your hat can find it."

We rode in silence, obeying rules and whistling along with the radio when a prowl car pulled up alongside. I caught occasional glances of my passenger in the rear-view when we stopped at traffic signals or passed some well lit bars that brought him out of the darkness, and I wished I hadn't. He had two slits where his eyes should have been and he was very young and muscular. He was packing a Luger for a road map and I followed it blindly. We got to my place and walked on up to my room. Of course, Mrs. Geetus never woke up when you wanted her to. If only I hadn't paid her that rent money, she'd be waiting at the door for me right now.

He told me to sit down and the way he watched me told me he was no stranger to this sort of business and that he could take me out of the picture any time he wanted to.

"Friend, you carry a lot of trouble with you. What were you doing eyeballing Joe's place tonight?" I assumed his sounding like Humphrey Bogart as Duke Mantee was as natural as it was intentional.

He was a lot bigger than I had thought, especially facing me, especially with the Luger pointing at my gut and his finger wrapped all tight and businesslike around the trigger. A siren wailed before I could answer. Even an average Joe could tell it was a couple of blocks away, but he got nervous and went to the window for a look see. He passed in front of me just that much too close and bam, I had him. He was on the floor and I was on the gun, returning to my feet with a smile and a well chosen, "Now it's your turn to do some talkin', chum. Who sent ya? And whattya want with me?"

He got up, placed his hat back on his head, ignored my smile, my invitation to chat, and his gun in my hand and walked out the door.

I laid down on the bed wondering how we both knew I wouldn't shoot him. I was on my second smoke before I realized that the whole thing had been too damn easy. I went out in the hall, opened the window and took the fire escape up to the roof, walked slow and easy across about half a dozen connecting roof tops and slid the Luger into the bottom of Lumpy Lombardi's pigeon coop, then retraced my steps just as quietly.

It was only about ten minutes after I was back in the sack that two burly dicks from the 83rd precinct busted in the door without so much as a knock or a how do you do. Their guns were drawn and when they said, "Don't move." I took it for granted that they omitted the "or else" because deep down they were really hoping I'd reach for something that would justify their trigger happy desires. I laid motionless on the bed and told them my piece was in the old Coldspot, second shelf, in the empty Corn Flakes box. I watched them as they checked the serial number against the one on my license. I swear their lips moved. Not satisfied, they tossed every piece of junk I had into the middle of the room. Then it was my turn. I landed with a thud on the old Zenith radio, and guessed by the sound of smashing-tubes that it wouldn't be telling me the scores of anymore Yankee games. Old Joltin' Joe's records would look just as good in the Daily Mirror, I figured. And I'd get to see what celebrities Winchell was batting around as a bonus.

The mattress glanced my right ear. Thankfully, you could see through the springs to the floor.

"Awright, Parker. Where is it?"

"Where's what?" I was as nonchalant as a man sitting on the floor, having furniture heaved at him could be.

"Let loose of that, 'where's what?' stuff or I'll hose you. You know what that's like, don't you, Harry, boy?"

"I can't give what I don't got, boys. Just tell me what it is you're looking for and I'll be glad to help you find it."

My ribs were introduced, several times, to the front of a Thom McCann black oxford, Size Eleven I believe, as they took one more look around the joint. I was beginning to think I should be a shoe salesman for the amount of leather this guy was throwing at me.

"What's this all about, fellah's?" I tried in my most friendly, innocent approach, still seated in the middle of all my worldly possessions.

"Just remember we'll be watching you, Parker." The older, tougher, size eleven bull said.

"Tell the guy who sent ya, it didn't work," I guessed.

"How did he. ... " the younger, less experienced brain started but was shoved out the door by the older bull who looked at me and said, "Wise guy, huh?"

As I was straightening up the joint there was a knock at the still slightly ajar door. Doc Cutter walked in, took a look around and said, "You weren't at Farrell's when I went back, but I can see now there was no reason for concern."

"No, just a little domestic situation, maid's year off," I said before filling him on the details of the night's visitors. "What've you got for me?"

"You were right. I think. About your man not being a crook that is. It's T.M. Collins' finger."

"So why do you only think? That's Mr. Wall Street you're talking about, not Mr. Dillinger."

"Yeah. Could also be 'Mr. Insider Information,' which ain't exactly the height of legality." He picked up my ashtray, looked around and realized there was nothing to place it on still standing, and put it back on the floor with a lot less enthusiasm than his predecessor.

"You think an after hours joint over on Sterling Place might still be open, Doc?"

He looked at his watch, which probably coincided exactly with the big clock at the Naval Observatory, mulled it over a second then said, "Don't see why not, it is after hours. You got something going over that way, Harry?"

"Gotta take a little ride. Couple of people named Ruby and Phil might still be there and I'll bet they're just dying to see me again."

"Well, in that case why don't I take a ride on over with you?"

"No, Doc. Not that I wouldn't enjoy your company. Just that this ain't no fingerprint job."

He said okay without any sign of being insulted, picked up Suzy, who had used up another of her nine lives by managing to stay in one - two pieces through the entire ordeal, placed her back on the table that I had just righted, and started for the door.

"Look Doc," I said, "by the time I'm through tonight it will be too late to get in touch with Cudge. Think you can do me a big favor and go back to Farrell's and see if he got anything for me? I'll see you at the lab first thing in the morning."

"Okay, Harry. Sure thing. Patty Bags drove me over in his car and we'll go back to Farrell's together." Patty was one of the few good ones left at the 83rd. We had worked a lot of midnight to eights together in our rookie days. He was a sergeant now, and smart enough to steer clear of Kaminsky and the like. The excitement in Doc's voice was enough to let me know that he believed he had been given a mission so important that the outcome of the entire case might turn on it.

CHAPTER 6

I wasn't surprised to see the 83rd precinct car so far out of its sector when I pulled up in front of Joe's Place. But it did put more than a damper on my questioning capabilities when Ruby and Phil came out together and got in the back of the squad car to be driven off by none other than Size Eleven and The Brain. I followed anyway feeling pretty confident that neither one of them would pick up on the tail. But when the boys got to 65th Street and let Phil and Ruby off at the same apartment building and Size Eleven turned off the ignition, scrunched down behind the wheel and put a thermos of steaming hot something or other up on the dashboard, I knew my night was through.

Something was up. Something I couldn't put my finger on. It didn't add up that Ruby and Phil had anything going and it also didn't figure that they were both in the same rent bracket. I stared at the apartment for about another hour, but it didn't do anything suspicious so I figured Ruby and Phil could wait until morning to hear what questions I had for them. I had been on enough stake-outs, both on and off the force, to know the boys were planted firmly for the night. Most people have no idea that the main ingredients of a stake-out are boredom, strong coffee, stale doughnuts and watching the clock tick in slow motion with the harsh realization of all the time being stolen from your life.

There was nothing left for me to do but go home and pour myself that extra large bourbon I had been promising myself since my mystery friend with the Luger had gotten the drop on me.

CHAPTER 7

WEDNESDAY, JANUARY 8TH

I woke up a little more unsteady than usual. By the time I had finished my Corn Flakes I noticed I had received another note. This one had been slid under my door, which meant the delivery boy was good enough to get past Mrs. Geetus. Sounded a lot like old second story Charles to me. Either he was employing the same quiet as a mouse technique he used while waiting outside doors at his master's house, or Mrs. Geetus was now in her room chopped into many pieces. Knowing Mrs. Geetus I decided a check of her room would not be necessary. I read the note, which was, of course, from that great word economist J.E. Collins.

Have you made penetration yet

She seemed stuck on five worders. I thought about it for a minute and remembered when she dropped in on me in Syd's, she had said, "Well, at least be good enough to let me know if you penetrate the identity of my father's captors." I could see I was going to have to devote some time to figuring out these little pearls of wisdom if they kept coming. And I knew they would keep coming. Since they were certainly no help with the case, I expected that continuing to ignore them would be my most prudent course of action. So I knew that this one, as well as its predecessors, would be better served elsewhere and on my way out slid it under Mr. Bellem's door.

It was a very shaky drive over to the lab. Even with the one eye opener the world was way too bright before noon. The 83rd seemed further away than usual, and after insuring that it was too early for Riles to be around, I went on in. The steps to Doc's basement lab felt steeper, harder on the knees.

"Hey, Doc. What's cooking?" I startled him to alertness. Not a usual reaction. "You didn't forget I was coming, did ya?"

"Nah. Just didn't expect to see you here, Harry. You got more moxie than a naked bull fighter."

"Look, Doc, I might be a little hung over, but didn't I say I'd be here this morning?" He was sedately looking at something pink and gooey on his desk. Something, I could tell just by the smell, I didn't want identified.

"Didn't expect you to keep that appointment after what happened last night." He looked at me for the first time since I'd entered.

"What happened last night, Doc?"

"Are you giving me the square, you don't know?" A hint of hope changed his face for the better.

"Cross my heart and hope Kaminsky dies." I made the sign of the cross and a silent wish.

He handed me the morning Journal. I read the headline and glanced a small piece of the story, but I really didn't need too many words. The glaring, in perfect focus, front page picture told the whole thing. Ruby and Phil laying on top of a squad car. What the words did fill in was that the two on top of the car worked together in a bar on Sterling Place. Also, that the driver, who I knew was Size Eleven, was in critical condition. The passenger, a.k.a. The Brain, had been killed along with the two "jumpers." "Apparently some sort of lovers suicide pact."

"And you think I had something to do with this, Doc?" I asked in disbelief, lowering the paper to get a better look at him.

"Ruby and Phil, just dying to see you again, from a bar on Sterling Place and this ain't no fingerprint job. Merely a coincidence?"

"Of course it's no coincidence. They're the two I told you about. The two I followed. But the two bulls in the squad car drove them there and planted themselves in front of the building. I couldn't even get in to question, let alone kill them. Damn, last night I couldn't figure why these two were together. It must have been for a meet with someone else and that someone, Doc, is who is pulling the strings and is who killed them. If only I had stuck around and seen who the hell came out of that building."

"I really knew it couldn't have been you, Harry. I just had to hear it from you's all. But why didn't you stick around?"

"I guess I was still thinking about the pro who waylaid me and set me up for a fall I just missed taking."

"The boys who came to your room last night?"

"You got it. No accident good old Size Eleven and The Brain showing up just after my young friend happened to leave his piece behind, or their being the ones to pick up Ruby and Phil and take them on their last ride. And I'll bet that piece is hotter than a firecracker and that it was left behind by some rookie cop that they were 'breaking in' to the ways of the job. Which reminds me I better give Lumpy a call before the day's out and tell him to clean out his pigeon coop. Now let me ask you something."

"Sure, Harry."

"Did you honestly believe a sector car from the wrong precinct just happened to be driving under their window as two 'lovers' decided to take their fateful leap?"

"I really missed that one didn't I, Harry? Hey, I'm sorry, what do you want, blood?"

"Yeah."

"What?"

"Well, see what you can come up with on Ruby and Phil for me. See who they were, if they had records and the like. I suppose it wouldn't hurt to see what you can find out about the two bulls while you're at it."

"The cops, Harry? What do you want to know about two cops?"

"Who they were assigned to for openers. After that, anything else you can think of. You know the angles, don't let that missing the car in the wrong precinct thing get you down, you're a damn good cop when it comes down to it." I wasn't just blowing smoke to make him work harder, I really respected the way the guy went about his job. And, in light of some past indiscretions, I was even willing to ignore the fact that he thought I could have killed Ruby and Phil.

"This may take a few days or so. None of the work's being done here. It was all sent over to the downtown lab. Strange thing, can't remember any other cases being handled that way before." He seemed to be mulling it over for possible answers as he spoke.

"Okay, Doc, you get to work on filling in the facts on our four friends. I got some calls I have to make."

I headed over to Syd's. Not surprisingly there were no messages and the Collins case was still the only one on my calendar. I handed Syd a quarter for five nickels and dropped an old buffalo into the slot and got Cudge on the horn. I asked him to see who had the juice to send lab reports clear across town to be analyzed, though I had a pretty good idea that the initials were going to come up John Mason.

"Harry, this is very embarrassin' to say, but even with all my contacts I ain't come up with word one on how the Collins dame fished your name outta the hat yet. So consider this lab thing a freebie. I got a reputation here."

"Your work record has never been in question with me, Cudge, no freebies."

"Thanks, Harry," he said with no small amount of appreciation in his voice.

"Geeze!" I yelled into my end of the phone. "I forgot to tell Lumpy about the rod I dropped into his coop."

"Good old Lumpy, keeper of Columba livia," Cudge said calmly into his end.

"Of what?"

"That's Latin, Harry. The English translation is Roch Dove. The Brooklyn translation of which is pigeon."

"Oh. Why didn't you say so?"

"Just did."

Then he went right into. "Say did I ever tell you that there are seventy-three elevators in the Empire State Building?"

"No, but thanks for sharing that with me."

We hung up and I dropped another nickel in and let the phone on the other end ring six times before Lumpy climbed down from his roof top perch to give an out of breath, "Yeah ... ha-ha-who's this?" Lumpy should only know about a building with seventy-three elevators.

I filled him in on my visitors and my actions and after a wicked little laugh he told me not to worry about a ding, he knew a spot in the canal dat was just right for my little acquisition. "Hey, Harry," he said in a tone that hinted his breathing was returning to normal, "tanks a lot for not lettin' any a my boyds get loose." Lumpy was one of those real neighborhood guys, stick him with a hot cannon and he thanks you for not letting any of his pigeons fly the coop.

I hung up the phone, passing up the temptation to quiz him on Columba livia, and headed back to my office. I had lost a little more space to a shipment of M & M's, Planter's nuts and Wrigley's Spearmint gum, but the sweet smell made it almost worth it as I tilted back in my seat and stared at a very Perry Mason looking brown stain in the upper left hand corner of my window. His hair was mussed and he had a devious smile. There may have been a phone in his hand, held up to the side of his face visible from the backyard. He could have been calling someone to ship a body clear across town. It was just coming into better focus when something outside the window flew away and Perry looked more like Winston Churchill who, I was reasonably sure, had not put the grab on T.M. Collins.

I stared a little longer, dragging my way through a couple of smokes and Perry reappeared only inches from where he had metamorphosed into Churchill.

What are you up to, you lousy S.O.B, I thought as Perry's face got clearer and clearer, until only his motives were in doubt.

I must have dozed off because the next thing I knew I was staring straight at Syd and he was going on about the lady on the phone. Had to speak to me right away. All excited she is. I got up and sidled past the nuts and chips out to my booth. It was J.E. It was nice to know that she could not only find Syd's in person, but that she also knew how to use a phone book. The note had finally come, she said.

One million, in small bills. The private dick can drop it on the pier at the bottom of Sackett Street. This Saturday, midnight.

"What do you think, Harry," she said calm enough to get my worry up.

"I think for one thing, they know I'm working for you, and I don't like that one bit." I watched through the glass doors of the booth as Frank the "handy man" who lives on my block, picked up a Racing Form and sat in a booth with a cup of coffee and a ham and egg on roll. He made a couple of quick picks, circling them in pencil as he ate.

"How do you think they know about you?" Miss Collins broke my mental stride and brought me back to the fold.

"Tailing me. Tailing you. Tailing anybody who comes to see you probably. Maybe even disguised themselves as the vacuum cleaner salesman who came to see you a few days ago for all I know."

"The refrigerator repairman, you mean."

"Yeah right." It took me a couple of seconds then I said. "What!" in a voice filled more with anger than inquisitiveness.

"A few days ago, a refrigerator repairman was in. Charles had let him in and then gone out on an errand. Then later on in the day when I asked him what was wrong with the refrigerator he said, 'Nothing as far as I know.' When I asked him why he let the repairman in if nothing was wrong with the refrigerator he told me that he thought the cook had called for him."

"Only, of course, she hadn't called him."

"That's right. How did you know?" She really hadn't gotten it.

"Stay right there. I'm coming over. And don't say another word about anything, to anybody, until I get there." Syd couldn't even get a "where are you headed" out before I had run back to my office, grabbed my hat and coat and run out of the store.

It took me all of fifteen minutes, even with the afternoon traffic, to get there. I caught a break when she answered the door herself. "Charles is shopping," she said. "Never mind that now." I grabbed her and brought her out into the street, which she didn't seem to appreciate. Her head swiveled in every direction, bothered less by the cold than the fact she may actually have to see, or God forbid speak, to a common passerby. I asked her to think, carefully, and describe the repairman. It only took a few words to realize her description fit Size Eleven to a T. Somewhere there was a connection between Ruby, Size Eleven and T.M. Collins. And somewhere, I'd bet my fee, there had to be a microphone in the house.

"Where did he go?" I said with more than enough excitement in my voice.

"I don't know about you, Mr. Parker, but we keep our refrigerator in the kitchen." She gave me her best iceberg imitation.

"Very funny, J.E. But since I'd be willing to bet my one good eye there's a microphone planted somewhere in this very huge house of yours, probably somewhere where you do a lot of talking. I'll ask you to try to remember if he went anywhere besides the kitchen, like maybe someplace where you might spend a little more time." I hadn't appreciated her "I don't know about you, Mr. Parker. ... " attitude.

"Mr. Parker, Harry. I believe you're trying to frighten me and I don't care for it one bit," she said in a frightened voice.

"Miss Collins, Janet. If I were trying to frighten you I'd be telling you a little story about four bodies trying to meet through the roof of a police car. What I'm trying to do is find out who's listening in on your conversations, because then I'll know who grabbed Daddy. And you didn't think I knew what I was doing, did you?"

"Well, he did go in the basement. He said he had to check the power down there. A fuse box I believe. And then he went into the drawing room." Her face revealed enough concern to explain why she didn't inquire about the four bodies or their failed attempt to meet.

"Why did he go in the drawing room?" I asked as if I didn't know.

"He said it and the kitchen were both on the same line, or something to that effect."

I told her to be quiet and just go along with whatever I said once we went in the house.

"I can't be quiet and go along with what you say at the same time." Her fear had subsided into her usual smugness.

Figuring we were now about even I decided to let it drop. I smiled, opened the door for her, and with a slight bend of my back and a wave of my arm, I motioned for her to go back into the house.

The note was on a marble pedestal, just inside the foyer. It was next to a bust of some long forgotten writer, or composer, or someone who had probably been dead for at least a hundred years. She handed it to me as if it were a shopping list and I were being dispatched on an errand. She had read it exactly.

"One million, in small bills. The private dick can drop it on the pier at the bottom of Sackett Street. This Saturday, midnight."

It was made up of headline clippings and it was easy to tell the different newspapers involved by the size and style of type. The Mirror, the Journal, the Times, the Eagle and even the World Telegram. Whoever it was went to a lot of trouble to let J.E. know he was very careful, or very professional, or very well read.

"Who touched this besides you, and now me?" I asked J.E., holding the paper out in front of me.

"Well, Charles opened it. And John, of course, insisted on reading it."

"Yeah. Well, I'll give it to my friend at the lab, but I don't think he'll be able to get anything now." I carefully folded the paper with my handkerchief and stuck the whole wad in my pocket, reasonably certain that at least one of us had touched it to help lend some explanation as to why our fingerprints were going to be found on it.

I knew the way to the drawing room and led on. Perry awaited within. I put my finger to my mouth in quieting gesture and began my search.

"There's no question about it, Miss Collins, the only thing to do is pay up." I tried to keep my voice at a normal volume, not wanting to tip off whoever was listening that I was on to them.

"I agree, Mr. Parker, but are you sure I'll get my father back if I pay?" J.E. had the volume raised to amateur theatrics pitch and level. My guess was that she had not participated in many school plays.

I stopped my quiet searching under pillows and in lamp shades long enough to give her a meaningful "Just go along, remember?" look and accompanying hand gestures.

"I'm sure if you don't pay you won't get him back," I said with a little more punctuation in my voice as I looked under the gold embossed just too divine divan. "These people obviously know what they're doing." I stalled for time, thinking over the basement and kitchen possibilities when I saw the wire running up the plush, royal blue drapes, tucked very professionally into a deep pleat. The microphone was located just below my shoulder, her mouth, height. I pointed to it and smiled with an all-knowing pride in my detecting abilities smile. John Mason, college graduate, with some pretty impressive initials after his name, I'd be willing to bet, came over and gave one quick jerk, pulling the mike to his chest with much bravado. He smiled, satisfied with himself as the wire cascaded through the drapes and hit the floor.

"Now," he said, "we may speak unencumbered."

"Now," I said, "you've taken away any possibility of our throwing a bluff their way. But I suppose, of course, that idea never crossed your mind, hey, Perry."

"See here, Janet, I don't care for his inferences to my deliberately subterfuging any stratagem of fraudulence you and he may have 'cooked up' while out of my ear shot. Don't care for it at all."

"Well if subterfuging stratagem of fraudulence means 'screwed up' you did it in spades, Perry, Darling."

"I will not have you use that language in front of Miss Collins. And I do not care for the constant use of 'Perry' either, Mr. Parker, and if you intend the use of 'Darling' as an aspersion to my manhood, then perhaps we'd better step outside this minute."

He had more in him than I'd given him credit for and I was just about to find out exactly how much when Miss Collins stepped in between us. She raised both her hands and suggested we would both be better off concentrating our efforts on finding her father rather than trying to prove which one of us was more adept at the childish pursuit of fisticuffs. Normally I wouldn't let a little thing like common sense get in the way of knocking some rich clown on his duff, but the lady had some very persuasive eyes when she cast them at you from just the right angle.

"Mr. Parker, what is your next move?" she asked coolly.

"By that, Miss Collins, I take it you mean what's my next move now that this golden opportunity has been clutched from my grasp?" My voice was neither calm nor low.

"No, Mr. Parker, I mean simply what is your next move?" She was as icy as the blue of her eyes.

I looked at Mason. "Nothing I'd wish to discuss at the present moment."

"Precisely as I suspected. The man has no clue of what to do next. A typical charlatan." His courtroom manner had been replaced with high pitched emotional intonation. He was losing it.

"Mason, if you listen carefully I think you'll be able to hear an ambulance with your name on it." I shook another Camel from its pack and smiled as sarcastically as possible. Mason walked back and started examining the drapes, probably for loop-holes.

CHAPTER 8

As I left the Collins joint I realized that it was still too early in the day for anything important to be happening, and despite his feelings on the subject, I figured it was time to drop Cudge another fin. On the drive over I realized he never truly appreciated his importance as leg man for most of my cases. His three room walk up on 43rd Street was permanently filled with cigar smoke. The smell of which attacked the olfactory organs whenever he opened the door. He smoked those short, dark brown, stubby jobs that most people in Brooklyn, even Italians, called guinea stinkers. They were god-awful to look at but the smell was ten times worse. And Cudge soaked them in brandy and let them dry a week or two, just for that extra added attack on the senses. The odor clung to the walls, carpets and furniture. He had a dog once, but it couldn't take living there, even with the free meals and occasional beers thrown in.

He motioned me in and gave me a big, "Gee, Harry, good to see ya," at the same time. And I knew with him it wasn't just a figure of speech. He shoved a few newspapers onto the floor, clearing a spot for me at the table and took a cold one from the fridge and passed it to me as I sat down. It occurred to me that in addition to all the people he spoke with on a daily basis he did an awful lot of reading. He handed me the church key and I used it as he moved some more papers and climbed into the chair opposite me. He balked a little as I slid the fin across the table, in that low gravelly voice that even he knew could never be disguised. It was the kind of voice that when raised could drown out a Dorsey orchestra: Jimmy, Tommy, or both. He took the fin and shoved it in his pants pocket and slid me another Rheingold in the same motion. We drank in silence for a while, listening to our lives ticking past on his Big Ben wind up alarm clock. It wasn't a pretty sound so I pierced it by asking if he had anything on the lab switch job, knowing full well it was too soon for him to have scared up a lead.

"No, Harry," he said. "Want your fin back?"

"Cudge, we're friends here. You've earned more than that already. Besides, I was just talking to hear myself. Sometimes it gives me ideas."

"Yeah, I know what you mean. I do the same thing sometimes, only usually when I've been drinking. Hey, did you know on May 1st, 1931, when the Empire State Building opened, President Hoover, way over in Washington, pressed a button and the tower lit up?"

I swear his chubby face glowed brighter than the tower lights at midnight every time he imparted another Empire Fact.

"How about some gin rummy? Penny a point," he said, and at the end of a couple of hours I was feeling pretty low, having my fin plus another back in my hand. Odds were if there was such a thing as a professional Gin Rummy Tournament that Cudge would never make it to the finals.

I put both fins back on the table and he looked at me like he was about to go into the enforcing end of his profession when I said, "It's another job, Cudge. You know I ain't no charity giver. I need info on insider trading, like maybe if T.M. Collins or John Mason or both are involved in it. This is definitely a sawbuck job, these people can play pretty rough."

He agreed without argument, which kind of worried me. I didn't think Cudge thought many people were worth a sawbuck to look into. Especially not socially polite gadflies whose biggest worries seemed to revolve around finding a good polo pony or a trustworthy upstairs maid. Trustworthy meaning not telling Mommy what Daddy is doing to her, I suppose.

We shook hands, and I walked down the dreary marble stairs passing the dark brown doors with the gold painted D1 - D2, C1 - C2, B1 - B2, and smelling the appetite-inducing aroma, of all day Italian cooking. By the time I hit the first floor I was wondering why the genius who owned the dive didn't just save himself some paint and time and number the apartments one through eight. I was also thinking about how long it would take me to get to Tony's over on Eighth Avenue for a plate of pasta and a bottle of red. A quarter of a cigarette later I was on the pavement staring at the cars drifting by and some old guy washing the dirt off his sidewalk with a green snake of a hose. January in New York is never warm enough to be hosing down a street and this one was no exception. Some of these old guys will do anything to keep busy. I walked up the street looking at all the gates wrought with iron and wondering if the old guy even realized what month it was.

I took a slow saunter to the office. Thinking that a couple of mile walk in the middle of January might be just the trick to clear some of the cobwebs of the case from my overcrowded with suspicions head. All it got me was a wind blown face and aching feet and the terrible realization that I was going to have to walk back and get the old Buick. As the candy store came into view I remembered that Cudge had once told me that a bad ride beats the hell out of a good walk any day. Right about now I was inclined to agree with him. Syd was out on his usual routine of trying to buy into some new taste treats that would guarantee every kid in the neighborhood would stop "Only here, after school."

Sarah would say, "He never exactly got stuck with anything but a killing he never made either."

Sarah was an enigma of mother, wife, shop-keeper and on days of my outright horniest, like today, of sexual intrigue. On days like this I would spend a little extra time up front helping out, mainly by watching her bend for something on the low counters, and wondering what she'd be like in bed. She was no looker, zaftig, I believe is the word Syd would use for her. It seemed as good a word as any. After about an hour or so I would realize I needed a date, real bad, and call one of the local ladies I had been seeing on and off for the past couple of years or so. I knew I was at that point now, but duty called so I went back to my office and tried to let the overwhelming sweet candied smell take me off in stained glass reflections of what the hell this whole case was all about.

Some kids with water guns. Where were their mothers, letting them play with water guns in January, had altered Perry's face to the point where I had to start looking for him elsewhere. Two old familiar clients, cases long since solved, had vanished into their

Tom Mix versus Hopalong Cassidy near window cleaning shoot out as well. The little varmints.

Well, I thought, the desk which was one of the few things I carried from the ashes of the Parlor Detective Agency, with its glass ring marks, heel scuffs and items thrown on it – had enough scars for me to try looking there for awhile. It took about ten minutes to realize that the desk could only display a faint reminder of my brother John. And I figured that was probably because I hadn't called him in about three months and was feeling pretty guilty about it.

John, the good brother as everybody referred to him when we were growing up, I guess because he stayed in school and out of trouble, was four years younger than me, with a wife, Maggie, a nice job in the stock market and three young kids. Jim and Jerry, were nine or ten, somewhere in that love-baseball-hate-girls stage and Joey, named after our father, was at that ceaseless energy, never running out of questions, pre-kindergarten age. They were really great kids who I occasionally took to Saturday movie matinees or Yankee games over at the Big Ballpark in the Bronx and overstuffed them with junk, just to the point where Maggie was thankful that I didn't come around more often. Deep down Maggie and I really liked each other, especially in the way we felt for John. Although she never said it I could tell she thought I was a bad influence on the kids. And who could blame her with Jim and Jerry always asking me if I had killed anybody new since the last time they had seen me and Joey always wanting to see my gun. It must have been hard for her to get them to put down their cap pistols for days after I left.

John's job, he did ... something on Wall Street, was okay, paid the bills with enough left over for some frills, but he certainly wasn't in any position to find out the kind of insider information stuff on the big shots that I was looking for. Not that I'd want to jeopardize it by asking him to poke around anyway, or that he'd even help me if he could. He made it very clear a few years back, when I first went private, that I was not to bring any of my work near his home. In fact he didn't want me stopping by when I was on a case. He had a family to think of and as usual he was doing a pretty damn good job of it. Prior to my taking on this Collins case I had a lot of time to stop by for a visit with the kids but hadn't and I guess that's what was really bothering me now that I was on a case and couldn't. Their Christmas gifts had been riding around in the trunk of my car for about a month now.

Looking down at the wooden card file box with its little dovetail joints reminded me of the meticulously kempt Mr. Mason. He managed to bother me whether his face came into view or not. The more I thought about him the more he seemed just the right type for kidnapping. He fit so right, like the perfectly fitted joints of the box that didn't even need glue or screws to hold them together. The kind of guy who would do anything to marry into millions. Who cared if J.E. was as frigid as an Alaskan winter and stayed cold twice as long, with that kind of dough you could buy babes by the dozens and stash them close by for a quick thaw now and then. A fifty million dollar neighborhood could have a babe around every corner and a corner every ten feet for all I'd ever know.

Syd came in, tired and disappointed. His latest confectionery quest had ended in failure. He plopped himself down in the chair opposite the desk.

"Just nothing new and exciting out there, Harry," he said. The redness of his cheeks not the only victims of the bitter cold.

I tried to imagine new and exciting candy and how one goes about being first to get "in on it." I pictured Syd in some back-alley, water front setting, with guys in trench coats "psst, pssting" him over.

"Hey, 'Candy Man,' right here, have I got a treat for you."

"No, here, 'Candy Man'. Here's the one that will make them come, 'Only to you, after school.'"

But the picture fell apart with Sarah's, "So, you found something or not?" coming from over his shoulder as he sat facing the desk.

"Or not," he said, defeat in his voice and the slouch in his shoulders like a back alley "psst" echoing in its own shadiness.

She waved both hands, palms out, to the side of her head. In sort of, "I could have told you" motion. Although he was facing me, his eyes rolling back in his head showed he knew just what emotion she was displaying. That, I guess, is part of the predictability of long term marriages. Without another word, she exited, turning her attention back to running the no new treats added, same old store.

"She can get like that sometimes," he said. "But other times ... " his smile and the rising pitch of his voice confirmed my earlier, Sarah bending to lower counter thoughts of what she must be like at "other times."

"Syd, you old dog," I said, knocking about five years off his age, if I was any judge of the male peacock pride sitting a little more erect and colorful opposite me.

"Harry, I think I'll close up a little early tonight." His eyes twinkled in anticipation.

"Yeah, Sydney, my man, why don't you do just that." I looked at my watch. Eight o'clock seemed as close to the truth as it was ever going to get. "I have to be heading out myself," I said.

"You be careful, Harry. That woman who came to see you the other day just looks like a lot of trouble to me. Money can't be spent if you're horizontal and at a level six feet below the closest bartender, you know."

"Thanks, Syd, I love you too."

"Love, Schmove. From who else would I get eight bucks a month for a space my cat wouldn't live in?"

"Remember that the next time I miss a month," I said with a wry smile. But his back was already to me as he hurried out to the store to wash everything down, close up early and go upstairs to share more than dinner with the zaftig Sarah.

CHAPTER 9

I had had enough walking and had taken the train back to my car. Now every light seemed rigged against me on my ride to Farrell's. As I opened the door I saw that Cudge was at the bar, telling somebody about fifty thousand feet of something that I just knew from the smile on his face had to do with the Empire State Building.

"Harry," he called, waving me over. "I've got some good news and some bad," he said as his new found friend dissolved back into the crowd. "How do you want it?"

"Haven't had much good lately, better give me that one first."

"Collins and Mason are both very definitely into insider stuff."

"Well, what can be bad news after that?"

"Name any other big name on Wall Street and I'll be able to give you the same info. And there is nothing yet that says Collins and Mason are into the same inside stuff, or that one even knows that the other's into it."

"Cudge, you found all this out, this quick, with only a sawbuck to work with?"

I tried to wave Joe the bartender over, away from some beautiful dame he was talking up, but he was having none of it. The dame was built like Phil and Ruby's fictitious blonde and was almost wearing a forest green, low cut, high slit number that got a rise out of my blind eye.

"They don't exactly keep secrets well down there when they think they're talkin' to a securities examiner," Cudge explained. "With the exception of one senior guy, who probably pulls down a bundle, I didn't have to spend a dime. In fact if I'd've had one more free cup of coffee I would have floated out of the joint. All ya gotta do is ask the right young guy who don't mind climbing his way up over a few bodies, and I swear they'd squeal on their own mothers. I'm afraid, Harry, the corporate youth of today has taken the word shame out of its vocabulary."

"Yeah, well, judging from your insider flash on Collins and Mason that may not only be the understatement of the year, it may apply to all generations."

"Harry, talk about takin' candy from a baby, all you got to do is find out a guy's wife's maiden name, check her bank account, and 'bingo' you've got his true assets. I mean these guys have no idea how easy it is to catch on to 'em. Or they know and they don't care because they also know that nobody's going to take a shovel to their accounts. With this info and the right buyers, I could bring down half of Manhattan."

I had to turn to the bar to prevent Doc from seeing the look I was trying not to throw at him. Those show tunes he always listened to were really starting to have a negative impact on him. I'd have to start slowly steering him to jazz.

"Yo, Joe! Three ... no, better make that six more Rheingolds over here."

Now Doc gave me a funny look.

"Who knows when I'll get his attention again, and don't thank me for the drinks. Thank Miss J.E. Collins."

"You are unscrupulous, Harry."

"Nonsense. You are providing me with information. She is providing me with an expense account. The twain have met." We threw our coats and hats on an unoccupied seat at our small table for four.

"In that case, if you don't mind, and because it ain't your dough, I did have to buy that one guy lunch today to get him to give over with the flash," Cudge broke in.

"What did it come to? Yours and his of course." I raised a generous hand to accent my benevolence.

"Four dollars and thirty-five cents. But that's with dessert and the tip."

"Here's a five spot, Cudge. Consider your lunch an official business expense."

"This private eye racket ain't half bad, Harry, I could get used to it in an awful hurry."

"Me too, Cudge, only there ain't enough T.M. Collins kidnappings to go around. Believe me."

"Hey, I know some guys, who could maybe put the snatch on some big dudes, then recommend that you take. ... "

"Never mind, Cudge, I'll just keep winging it, if you know what I mean."

"Could be easy bucks, Harry."

"The only easy bucks are the ones you spend, not the ones you have to earn."

"I hear that, Harry. Say did you know that the base of the Empire State Building is two square acres of solid concrete laid fifty-five feet below street level?"

"Really," Doc said, in true amazement. "I can't figure how you. ... "

I started thinking, as they carried on with their Empire State Fascinating Facts conversation. My thought grew louder and more annoying as I pondered where I was getting, or rather not getting with this case. I'm no closer than I was yesterday to finding T.M. Three people are dead, probably as a direct result of my questioning them, well, at least two of them, The Brain could have been an accident. Although he should have known better than to be parked in a yellow zone and sitting as damn erect as a drill sergeant at a full dress parade. If he had been slouched down like Size Eleven, or any normal guy after a full day's work, he might be alive today. He too, must have been the product of Catholic School, "Sit Up Straight!" ruler to the knuckles discipline.

I turned back to my cohorts. Their conversation ended, I decided to enlist their help.

"Mason wants J.E. T.M. objects but that angle just doesn't fit. As much as I'd like to cram his round hole into a square cell. I mean if T.M.'s returned after the pay off he's going to object to their marriage anyway. And we're not even sure that Mason needs the million. Or are we, Cudge?"

"Sorry, Harry, I didn't think to cover that angle. I'll have it for you first thing in the morning."

"Harry?" Doc's voice was interrogative.

"Yeah, Doc?"

"What if he doesn't?"

"Doesn't what?"

"Doesn't return T.M. after the pay off. He gets the million bucks and J.E." His worried look showed he had thought it through.

"Yeah, then whether he needs the million or not he gets what he really wants, J.E. and her money. And if he doesn't need the million it's an even better fit because he diverts suspicion from himself at the same time he's getting her. Doc, you're brilliant."

"Harry, I don't like this Mason guy much myself, but I haven't found his link to the cops yet." Cudge chinned in.

"So, what's your point?" I was trying not to let anyone burst my Mason's-the-one bubble.

"So maybe he shouldn't be your only suspect is all I'm sayin' here."

"Well, he's not my only suspect, Cudge. He's just the best one I got so far. I'm not forgetting Size Eleven or The Brain's part in this that fast. Not while I still got a sore rib to remind me of them. Charles doing a stretch for manslaughter because his ex-boss asked him to kill his wife doesn't exactly eliminate him either. And the fact we got a chopped finger and he likes to play with an axe is embedded deep in my mind. And don't think I'm thrown off by a beautiful face either ... well, not entirely, anyway. J.E.'s agreeing with Mason not to call the police in on this may mean that she has something to hide as well."

His slight smile said that he was pleased that I was at least attempting to keep an open mind on the subject.

"Holy hell! What was that?" somebody yelled as practically everybody else hit the floor.

"Those, my friend, were gun shots," I said in a calm voice, as I squatted under the table, with my beer held firmly in my hand, every drop contained in its bottle.

"No windows hit, Harry," Doc said from his position by my side.

"Nothing came in at all," Cudge added, firmly seated, serenely in his chair.

"Yeah, I know. Well, I figure enough time has passed for our shooters to have made their getaway. Let's go check around outside."

"Oh! No! Not again!" I stared at the water draining from the old Buick's radiator.

"People sure have a thing for that car, Harry." Doc couldn't hold back a grin.

"Maybe it's Vinny," Cudge threw in. "Could be how he stays in business. After all even you'd have to agree that you are his best customer, Harry."

"More likely a little warning, don't you think, guys? About as well disguised as a bleached blonde in a convent."

"Stay away or else, huh, Harry?"

"Right on the money, Doc."

"Guess there's nothing left to do but go home."

"Yeah, Cudge. Come on, I'll give ya. ... Hey, Doc, you think you could drop me and Cudge off on your way home?"

"Sure thing. What are you going to do about the old Buick, Harry?" My friend was genuinely concerned.

"Not much more can happen to it where it is. I'll leave it there for the night. In the morning I'll call Vinny and bill J.E."

"You're incorrigible, Harry," Doc said shaking his head like an admonishing finger wagging.

"Now, Doc, you can't honestly tell me that you think that the car getting shot had nothing to do with this case can you? I mean, let's let logic dictate here, it is the only case I'm working on. And if you take a look around you'll note it's the only thing that got hit."

"Well, when you put it that way. ... It just seems to me that you can always put it that way."

"That's just because I've got a business mind, Doc."

"Yeah, shady business," Cudge threw in as we climbed in to Doc's wagon leaving the old Buick bleeding its liquid onto the frozen street and hearing the first strands of a young Judy flying somewhere over the rainbow.

CHAPTER 10
THURSDAY, JANUARY 9TH

There's nothing in this world like Corn Flakes and milk after that first shot of bourbon in the morning. Unless it's ruined by a note slipped under your door. God, what time do these people get up? And why in the hell won't J.E. believe me when I tell her she isn't about to get instant replies to these damn things.

I let the note sleep a little longer on the floor, it looked tired and I felt like indulging myself in a second bowl of flakes. The luxury of steady employment.

Mrs. Geetus came in. I'm glad I've learned to sleep wearing at least my shorts.

"Lady on the phone for you," she said in her early morning husky voiced, abrupt fashion. "I don't appreciate calls this early in the day, Mr. Parker," she continued without a pause for my concern or for the note she'd just stepped on.

"Tell her I'm still sleeping, please, Mrs. Geetus."

"Mr. Parker! I am a member in good standing of the Saint Agnus Church of God. I do not lie. Kindly answer the phone and let this woman know that you are, well ... at least awake. Further, be so kind as to inform her that I do not appreciate her annoyances."

She watched as I walked to the phone, took the receiver and without saying a word hung it up.

I smiled broadly as I walked past her, picked out a towel from the tall, creaky drawer, dresser in the hall and moved toward the bathroom.

"If she calls back, Mrs. Geetus, you can, without fear of divine retribution, tell her I'm in the shower."

She walked off in what can only be described as a major huff and before I hit the bathroom I picked up the phone, called Vinny, and let him know what had happened to the old Buick Special and where it was. His laugh was even less appreciated than J.E.'s note and phone call. If mechanics who were willing to trust you without payment until your next case came along were easier to find I might think of taking my business elsewhere, I thought, as I let the water run extra hot while having some cold shower thoughts of Thelma.

When I got back to my room I picked up the note.

I saw the ugly photos

It took me a minute to realize she meant the pictures of Ruby and Phil in the newspapers. Somewhere back in her past she must have given lessons on how to write telegrams. Five words - stop.

I thought it was smart of her to connect the pictures to my telling her of four bodies trying to meet through the roof of a police car. I wondered if she had called me to tell me she saw the pictures or to ask me if I had found out anything new last night.

Who was I kidding. It was to demand if I'd found out anything new. I could hear my voice telling her, "Yeah, J.E. I found out your father and your ... whatever, are both crooks, involved in insider trading and that someone has some kind of strange hatred for the old Buick, which by the way will set you back about another fifty or sixty bucks." But I knew, more than likely, I'd just tell her about the car, maybe throw in an, "And I'm following up on another lead that's just too early to discuss at this point." I thought about it. That might only get three or four more notes so maybe just sticking to the car angle would be best for now.

If my memory had any trust left in it, it seemed to me that Cudge had told me that he'd be out all morning so I decided to see what Doc Cutter was up to, but first I had another note to drop off. Delivering mail to the mailman was getting to be such fun. I wonder if Mr. Bellem gets this good feeling every day delivering his mail.

I walked down to the train station on Smith and 9th and took the local over to the 83rd. I had a fight with one of those stuttering doors that couldn't make up its mind and got caught in the middle while I was trying to get off. Some guy in greasy, machine shop work clothes got a yelling fit, like I made the door grab me or something, but then what else is new in the subway.

"I'm glad you're here, Harry. I was going to call you but I didn't have your number."

"It's in the book, Doc." He's known me for more years than I care to remember. Yet now that I think of it, he had never called me at home before. I couldn't remember ever calling him either.

"I didn't see any Harry Parker listed," he said.

"It's under Geetus, Pearl."

He gave me one of those looks that said, he realized that he had screwed up plainer than any language ever invented.

"Don't sweat it," I said, "there's not a better man in a lab than you anywhere in this country. I'd stake my life on it."

"Thanks. You know I was first in my class at. ...

"Doc." I interrupted.

"Yes, Harry?"

"What were you trying to get a hold of me for?"

"Oh, yeah, that. To let you know Rogers died this morning. Word came over the teletype to the precinct upstairs."

"Damn, I can't catch a break on this case."

"Neither can Rogers."

"Yeah, well, at least his worries are over. If I don't get off my duff, Mr. T.M. Collins may never catch another break either. I'm going to see if I can hunt down Cudge, Doc. I'll catch you later, over at Farrell's."

"Wait, there's more."

"More what, Doc?" He caught me at the bottom of the steps, just getting ready to take them at double time.

"More bad news," he said slow and uneasy.

"Why the face? It can't be worse than Size Eleven croakin' can it?"

"It's worse, much worse." He had that downward cast to his eyes that people use when they don't want to tell you something that they know they're going to have to.

"Well, what the hell is it, Doc?" I pulled up a chair and took the prerequisite seat to receiving disturbing information.

"Steve Taylor's dead too, Harry."

"Yeah, so give me the bad news?" Laughter was not far from escaping my mouth, bad taste or not.

"They're holding Thelma for it." His voice had gone so low I had to strain to hear him.

"Thelma. You gotta be kidding me!" I yelled, my voice booming in unbelieving contrast.

"No. They found the gun he was killed with and it was registered to her. I checked on it myself, Harry. There were no prints at all on the gun. And, according to the report she doesn't remember it leaving the apartment. The neighbors, of course, were questioned and the only damned thing they could all agree on was that

Thelma and Steve fought like cats and dogs. And that is a direct quote from at least three of the nosey biddy sources."

I sat quietly for a minute or two, my first thoughts I'm ashamed to admit were happy ones at the news that Thelma and Steve were not getting along. Then I remembered that I had given Thelma that gun when we were still married. I was still on the force then and was worried that some of the bad boys I had put away might come looking for me. A cop's shift changes all the time and wives without weapons can be easy targets for punks who think raping, or beating women evens the score or somehow makes them look like the men they will never be.

"It's still all circumstantial, Doc," I said in a shocked to whisper voice. "Not a bit of solid evidence in the whole damn thing." I tried to be more convincing sounding but wasn't even getting myself to believe it.

"Maybe not, but they've got motive, opportunity, the weapon and the body. Circumstantial or not, you know as well as I do how all that is going to play to a jury."

I stood for a minute, knowing all too well how all that would add up to a jury. My heart started beating a lot harder. My palms were sweating. I hadn't felt like this since ... since the last time I had had anything to do with Thelma. "I'm going upstairs, Doc, to see what the hell's going on. You know who's handling the case?"

"Yep."

"Who?"

"Kaminsky." He delivered it without any particular reading. The one word said all it had to.

"Oh, great. As if my life didn't have enough complications." Somehow my legs got me off the chair and headed up the steps.

The inside of the 83rd precinct smelled about the same as all the others I'd ever spent any time in. Stale, and musty. Like old tuna fish, and acrid urine that permeates through the nostrils after one whiff and lingers with you long after you've left the place.

"Where's Sergeant Kaminsky's office," I asked Conners, the desk sergeant who had been a fixture in that seat for more years than anyone could remember.

"Lieutenant Kaminsky now, Harry. Just as big an a-hole as ever though. Second floor, rear, he's got Homicide." He almost looked as amazed saying it as I did hearing it.

"Well, at least all the murderers in the neighborhood are safe," I cracked.

"You got that right," he said, after checking that no one was within ear shot. "Want me to announce you?" He reached for the switchboard.

"No thanks, Pappy. Bernie just loves surprises, if I remember correctly." I didn't want him to have enough time to prepare a goon squad before I got to the second floor.

He shook his head knowing my motives, put the receiver back in its cradle and went back to his Police Gazette and his half eaten banana.

Rogers dead, Thelma charged with a murder and Kaminsky a lieutenant, I thought. My God, could my day get any worse? I took the back steps to the second floor. The fragrance didn't improve with altitude. The door to Homicide was slightly opened. Two voices spilled out into the hallway. Bernie's high pitch shrill hadn't matured with the passing years. The other box was vaguely familiar but I couldn't quite place it. I opened the door all the way without knocking and Bernie and Bill Riles, one tough nut case with a chip the size of a redwood on his shoulder stopped jawing as soon as they saw me, which took them a minute or so. They were such great detectives, these two. Kaminsky had no doubt brought Riles over to Homicide for his expert phone book interrogation technique.

"Now, see, Sergeant Riles, I win. I told you old Harry would have the ... errr, courage to come calling."

Riles fished a fin from his pocket and slid it across the desk to Bernie. His look was anything but one of joy and I would have loved to get a bet down myself. I'd bet this wasn't going to be the last I'd hear about Riles' five bucks.

"Now thank the nice man for losing you our bet, Sergeant. And after you just had that big moving bill out to Bay Ridge too." Good old predictable Bernie was always a great one with grammar and at pouring gasoline on fires.

"Gee, thanks, Parker. Maybe I can return the favor someday, real soon." Riles' smirk told me I was going to lose a lot more than a five spot before my day was done.

"Like to speak to Thelma, Bernie," I tossed out casually.

"Sure you would, Harry, I can understand that. I was just saying that to Riles here, only you know procedure. Unless you got something in writing from the D.A. - You ain't got no D.A. paperwork with ya - do ya, Harry."

"No, Bernie."

"Then you got to speak to us first. Ain't that right, Sergeant?"

"Sure as hell is, Lieutenant. Officer in charge of a murder investigation has to grant permission, in writing, for a. ... Say Parker, what form of visitor are you in this case. A private dick, or a caring ex-husband?" They both let out little chuckles, probably as much mirth as they were capable of without a beating going on.

"A little of each. But that doesn't really matter much to you, does it, Riles?" I wasn't enjoying myself.

"See, Lieutenant, just when I was tryin' to make all nice and friendly, your old pal here cracks wise. Now I ask you, what's a guy to do?"

"Well, Sergeant, I suggest we start by asking Mr. Parker to take a seat so we can see exactly what's on his mind. And what exactly his relationship is to the accused." There was enough sugar in Bernie's voice to throw a diabetic into shock.

I sat in the seat facing the desk. Riles, showing a bit more neck vein than when I walked in, slithered behind me and closed and locked the door.

"Now just what went wrong with you and Thelma, Harry, if you don't mind my askin', that is?"

"Oh, I don't mind your asking, Bernie, as long as you don't mind my not answering."

Riles slid his foot under the back legs of my chair and jerked my shoulders back so fast I was checking the cracks in the ceiling before I even knew I'd hit the floor. This was a tactic I had used myself. You hope that the poor slob you're ... questioning gets mad enough to hit you back, then you arrest him for assaulting an officer. All his bruises and fractures incurred up to and from that point on then go down on the official record as "inflicted while trying to subdue."

"What was that question again, Bernie?" I said without bothering to get back up.

"You, Thelma, split, why?"

"Let's just say she was the kind of girl who liked climbing into other men's laps, even when they were standing up, as the old story goes."

"Yeah, I've heard that one a few times. And how did the split up finally come?"

"I just went home one night and found I had some more closet space and a lot more room in bed."

"Then how come you made her a present of a gun?"

"Flowers just never say enough."

Riles could only kick me in the ribs. My master plan of not getting back up had foiled his tactic of knocking me back down again. Sometimes it's the little victories that mean so much. I smiled up at him from my new flipped over position of floor tile inspector. But Bernie's question about the gun had hit its mark. He had let me know that Thelma had told him that I had given her the gun, thus giving him exactly what he wanted, my involvement.

"Oh, Harry, I haven't got time to play these games." Bernie sounded absolutely exasperated.

"I know, Bernie, there are so many murders, and so many innocent people that somebody has to pin them on. Not to mention that today is graft collection day."

Riles used a black leather soft sap this time. Behind the right ear. I must have been tiring him out. I rolled around a bit and had to admit he was good. A novice might have knocked me cold, spoiling any future fun.

"Bernie, unless Bill here needs the workout," I looked at Bill smiling above me, "which I can't imagine to be the case, why don't we cut to the I get to ask you a question portion of our little game?"

"Go right ahead, Harry, only please don't upset the Sergeant here any further. He's been very polite so far, but I'm afraid he's on the brink of losing his temper."

"Did you run a paraffin test on her hands to see if any nitrate particles showed?"

Bernie nodded and Riles smacked the back of my head. No doubt about it I was wearing him down.

"That one, Harry, assumes we're stupid. There were no prints on the gun so the shooter wore gloves, what's a paraffin test gonna prove? Try to be more careful if you have any other questions, Harry. I'm afraid Bill here is a little sensitive to his intelligence being questioned by some fly-by-night private peeper who keeps his brain between his legs." I wisely bit my tongue on the issue of his intellectual prowess, or lack of same.

"Bernie, you know unless they were real thick gloves a paraffin test will reveal something just the same."

He nodded again. I covered my head. Riles kicked me in the ribs, hard. I may have been overconfident in my last assessment of the fatigue factor.

"Once again, Harry, you assume we do not know our jobs. This upsets Sergeant Riles very much. Any more questions?"

"Do I get to see her, or not!"

Riles hit the same rib as Size Eleven this time and it hurt like hell.

"What was that one for," I managed to squeak out in a voice I'd never heard before.

"Phrasing," Bernie said plain and simple, "counts twenty percent to your overall score. You must ask your questions more politely, Harry."

"You know what, fellahs? Why don't we just call it a day? Forget I ever came in here."

"Oh, Harry, you mean after all our polite chatter you don't want to see your ex-wife anymore? I am surprised." Bernie's sarcasm was as thick as molasses.

"Say, Harry. I got those pictures I took of you this morning," he said and waved a brown envelope at the room, "you want them here or sent to your place?" Good old Doc Cutter, cut in with a perfect reason why Kaminsky and company had better not inflict any more bodily harm on me. His years in the 83rd had dulled his senses to the sight of my prone position, or he was just too much of a friend to bring the matter up.

"Send them to my place, Doc, I think I may be needing them after all."

"Harry, don't you think you ought to be going? It's been a long day and that fall you took as you came in here can't be helping that old back injury of yours any." Bernie, the track coverer was quickly at work.

"You're right. Sorry if I ruined your day or something, Bernie."

"Oh, no, no. On the contrary, Harry. Stop by again, sometime. Sometime we can spend a little more time together. We've had such a nice day today. Too bad you have to leave so soon."

I picked my hat and myself off the floor and headed for the door. With the bravery of Doc and his envelope I gave Riles a little shove as I passed him.

"Harry," Bernie said coolly, and I turned slowly, suspecting Riles had at least one more low blow, sucker punch in him.

"Yes, Bernie."

"Thelma went home hours ago. Her brother posted her bail." They both snickered. The sucker punch had been delivered verbally.

"Thank you, Bernie. You've been most kind."

CHAPTER 11

W ith the exception of about five minutes at her mother's funeral, I hadn't seen Thelma since the night she and Steve took her clothes to his car. I had stood at the window, with the lights out for about an hour or so after they had pulled away from the curb. The rain came down in sheets the whole time and not one person walked by. The teeming sound was all that embraced me.

She looked damn good when her door opened.

"I knew you'd come, Harry. You were always such a sweet guy."

Even from an ex-wife that line sounded too much like "we can still be friends" to be anything but the slap in the kisser it was.

"Well, are you going to ask me in or do I ask you why you offed Steve from out here?"

"Maybe sweet wasn't exactly the word I had in mind. If you're here to help come on in. Gloating you can do in the cold." We moved into the small apartment and took chairs across from each other, avoiding the intimacy of the couch. "If you think that helping me in this means you and I got any shot in the world of getting back together just forget it and take the next Sea Beach out of Bensonhurst, Harry." She had opened the conversation on one of her warmer notes.

"Yeah, I missed you too, baby. Couldn't help but notice the Parker moniker over the bell."

"Bother you, Harry D a r l i n g?" She drooled out the darling with a sarcastic smirk of old.

"Why leave your maiden name disused? It once meant you. Parker was a lie you wore just long enough to tarnish, let it go. Give it back the respect it deserves."

"I only keep it to get free drinks at most any bar in Brooklyn." Her face had more glow than I cared for.

"You want my help or not?" A ship of the desert instinctively went to my mouth.

"Need, it's more like it. You're not much but right now you're all I've got."

"Gee, aren't you afraid such high praise will swell my head? I can't imagine why you need my help though. Steve was such a great detective. Too bad you can't get him to help you."

She broke down, burying her face in her hands, supporting the weight of my remark added to that with her elbows on her knees, bawling and trembling like a baby.

"Sorry, babe. That was a low blow, even for us."

"What happened to you?" she sobbed. "You look terrible."

"I asked Bernie Kaminsky what he had on you."

"In your usual winning way, I'm sure."

"Just like you. I get the shit kicked outta me tryin' to help you, and somehow it's my fault. Look, maybe this was a bad idea. I'm on a case right now and I don't know how much help I could be to you anyway, what with Bernie workin' the other end and all. I might actually be more harm than good."

"No. Wait! I mean, please stay. I really need you right now." Her voice had softened to something less than hatred.

It was an awkward minute or two before she finally spoke again.

"Coffee? Black, right? No sugar."

She didn't wait for my answer. She went into the kitchen and I watched what I'd been missing. Her walk in a tight skirt said more about sensuality than every drunk induced poet ever born. It was the kind of sight men fought crusades for. The English, off to war with the Infidels.

She came back after about a hundred years and handed me a cup. I recognized it as one of a set that had been a wedding gift from one of her relatives that I had thankfully long since managed to forget.

"What's the case," she said.

"Huh?" I dragged my eyes from the china mug to hers.

"The case. You said you were on a case." She took the seat she had vacated and put her cup and saucer on a butterfly table next to the chair.

"T.M. Collins," I said, and took a sip of her always great coffee.

"Are you kidding me?" Her voice showed a lot more shock than I'd cared for.

I'd have been insulted, or probably more like mad as hell if it weren't for the fact that I couldn't believe I was on the T.M. Collins case myself.

"What's the matter? You think I can't handle it? You think Steve could've done better?" Maybe I was a little mad anyway.

"No, that's not it. I was just wondering, why you?"

Yeah, so was I, but I wasn't about to admit it. Especially not to her. Especially not now when it seemed she needed me for a change.

"Sounds like the same thing to me. I can manage though, and throw your case in to boot."

"Oh, careful, Harry, you're beginning to sound like one of those cheap dime store novels."

"That's about where you rate me, ain't it, baby?"

"Aw, Harry, let's not go round and round again. What do you say?" Her voice was syrupy sweet and soft, like it was a million years ago when we first met.

"Suppose you tell me what happened?" I'd had enough cigarette and stamped it out in the small round ashtray I'd been using. It looked like it could only hold one cigarette at a time so I didn't bother lighting another.

"I don't really know. I mean I don't really know what happened to Steve. I came home from work last night and Steve was in bed. I figured he was sleeping and didn't say anything. I got undressed and when I pulled back the covers I saw all the blood. Funny, but I knew right away he was dead. I called the police and Bernie and Mr. Charm came over. They asked me a few questions, took me to the precinct, told me I was being charged with Steve's murder and kept me there till my brother, Freddy, bailed me out."

"You say you came home from work?"

"Yeah, Steve hadn't gotten any cases in over a year so I've had to waitress at some little joint over on Montague Street." She looked down, not being too proud, I supposed, of the fact that life with Steve had sent her out to earn the rent.

I tried not to let my overwhelming joy burst out. "Didn't the people at work say you were there. If Steve was killed before you came home, that would alibi you?"

"Yeah, but Bernie said they were just coverin' for me."

"He would."

"Besides, according to them he was killed just a little before I got home and I had done some shopping so they say there's some unaccounted for time."

"Was Steve fooling around?"

"What's a matter, Harry, don't you remember how good I was? You'd just love it to be that wouldn't you?" She had a lace handkerchief in her left hand and was twirling it around and around with her right.

"That ain't it at all. I'm just trying to see who, besides you and about anybody else who ever met him, would want to kill the lousy bastard's all."

"Sounds like you can put yourself down on that list," she spat.

"No, I just felt sorry for him," I lied.

"No, I don't think he was fooling around," she half whispered. She was no longer facing me, which made it sound even lower.

"Do you think he might have been working a case?"

"No. I told you he didn't have a case for over a year." She was facing me again now and some of the volume, if not feeling, was back in her voice.

"What were the last cases he had?"

"How the hell would I know. Why do you want to know that stuff, anyway?" The feeling had returned as well.

"Maybe somebody he put away just got out. I don't know. I'm fishing."

"Yeah, and I'm the bait."

"Wrong, honey, unless I can prove otherwise, you're the catch of the day."

"I really don't know. We didn't talk about his cases. He wasn't like you. He said he didn't like to talk about work because it might somehow get me involved."

"And you believed that. ... "

"Yeah, Harry, some people are like that. They don't want to risk hurting the ones they love." She gave me her full face and it was wearing a very disapproving look.

"Did you read that somewhere or did Father Purick map it out for you. 'Cause it seems to me you never had this true revelation before." I spoke with all the pain of her leaving rushing back at me like a defensive lineman sacking the quarterback of his wildest dreams.

"You want another cup of coffee, Harry? Your rhetoric is losing some of its punch."

"Naw. We've done enough sparring for one day. I got to get going. I'll take your case even though you didn't actually ask."

"Thanks, Harry. I was hoping you would." Both our voices had mellowed.

I went out the door and took a slow walk to the subway. I was headed to Cudge's house, hoping he was home. I had a whole new set of questions for him and I also hoped he had some old answers waiting for me.

The subway ride was slow and long, giving me too much time to remember our past. The uncomfortable ripped straw seats couldn't help stop the rumbling images. Countless tunnel lights flashed by in a blur as I sat thinking through the old Thelma and me times. Good times, when love was still a two way street with forever up ahead instead of a dead-end road.

When I got off the train and walked to Cudge's block the guy with the hose was nowhere to be seen but his sidewalk was clean and wet. A thin stream of water rushed bottle caps and bits of paper toward the corner sewer, so I knew he was still vigilantly doing his civic best.

I started up the dingy stairs only to see Cudge staggering down. He had been shot. Not bad, from what I could see. Ripped a small chunk of flesh off his right side. I got him down the stairs and into a cab and on over to Doc Dearborn's place. Doc patched him as best he could for a man who was concentrating so hard on giving me the needle.

"This's got to be your doing somehow," he said, with each stitch he sewed in Cudge's side and I guessed that he was right. Then he made me promise to check Cudge into the hospital, and have him examined for infection. He gave the name of a doctor friend of his who would, for a nominal fee, check him in as an appendectomy patient, even though the wound was on the wrong side. Then he handed me the bill. Cudge wanted to take it but I told him not to worry, I was charging it to J.E. Doc took it back and made a minor adjustment upward and smiled warmly thinking, I would imagine knowing him, of three quarts of Dewars and a little nurse from Pediatrics who had the greatest bed room manner.

I had kept the questions to a minimum on the way to Doc Dearborn's place. Now that he was patched up and we were taking a more leisurely cab ride to the hospital I was able to find out that Cudge had come home and surprised a guy in the process of tossing his apartment. He had made a lunge for the guy, but the guy had been quicker, sidestepping and firing before Cudge could set himself for the next attack. There was something ... he just couldn't put his finger on it, but there was something about the guy. At this point he had closed his eyes and I figured rest was more important than information. I knew that after I got him checked in I'd come back for a visit and maybe he'd remember then what the something was. I gave the name Dearborn had given me to a nurse sitting at her station on the first floor. A middle-aged guy with cold, dark features and a warm smile answered her page. After I told him who I was, who had sent me and deposited a fifty dollar cash payment in his soft, pink palm, he set the admitting procedures in progress.

By the time I got home, after getting Cudge settled in over at Brooklyn Hospital and then waiting for two trains, it was late afternoon. There were two handwritten messages from Mrs. Geetus regarding telephone calls from Miss Collins in the chair by the door. This was getting comical.

The second message had a little P.S. on the bottom. Mr. Parker, you owe me fifty cents. I am not a telephone operator.

I wasn't so sure about the telephone part.

I put the messages on the table and rested my weary back on the bed. I figured ten or fifteen minutes would put it back in place enough for me to get back up and throw a sandwich together. The back, and the eye, had kept me out of the fighting. I got them, or lost them, both at the same time. Back in '39 a Mobil gas station heist was called over the car radio. I saw the powder blue Plymouth headed down Atlantic Avenue and gave chase. He made the turn at the foot of Hicks Street. I didn't. The water was icy cold and a lot harder than you'd expect when diving into it from inside a police car. My head jerked forward with the impact and met the little metal clip that held the car radio phone with my right eye. The pain probably saved my life as it gave me enough strength and adrenaline energy to get the hell out of the car and swim to the pier before I collapsed and it sank.

Those injuries definitely would have gotten me thrown off the force before the Kaminsky incident. But by the time I was out of the hospital in early '40, the big downtown boys were already worrying about the possibility of losing all their experienced men to the impending war. So until my little blow up, I had remained part of "The Finest." The Plymouth and its occupants, as far as I know, are still doing fine. Although if I were a betting man I'd lay you eight to one that the occupants are probably on the inside, or dead by now for something else they'd done.

It was six o'clock when I must have tried to roll over, sending that old familiar nerve pinching numbness down my back through my ass cheek and into my left leg. The built-in alarm clock of strenuous days or rainy nights. My ribs had added an extra little twinge that now seemed part of the whole malady.

I forced myself over to the fridge and put a little of everything between two slices of bread. I had just taken a seat at the table when Janet Elizabeth Collins and John Perry Mason opened the door and waltzed on in. They both wore the same "don't let anything touch you" look on their upper crust mugs as they quickly shifted their eyes to take in the entire Parker estate.

"Now suppose you go back outside and try knocking," I said, "I ain't got no treasured antiques or gorilla butler, but this place is all I have, and I kind of like when people respect my privacy."

"Now see here. ... " Mason began, but I was tired, beat up and cranky and I was having none of it. I raised my .45 from its resting place on the table and waved them toward the door. I knew that they were both very good at charades because they stepped out without a word spoken, waited a second or two and then knocked very politely. I waited till they knocked a second time before I just about sang "ca-ome in-nnn." I was enjoying being on the winning end for a change.

"As legal counsel to Miss Collins I demand you show some semblance of evidence that you have not been taking her for a ride, as they say in your parlance. Some confirmation as to the facts that you have collected to date. And, I demand it, post haste."

"Very well put, Mr. Mason. Are you absolutely sure you want me to talk right now?"

"Absolutely."

"Very well then. For openers you owe me for my friend getting shot up. There'll be an emergency doctor and hospital bill on that. For another you owe me for my car getting shot up, radiator. There'll be a bill for that too. Oh, yes. I'm afraid there's another rather substantial bar tab as well." I dragged my ashtray closer and lit another smoke.

"Is that all you have to tell Miss Collins? And why do you expect payment for any of these entities without proof you have been providing the services contracted for?"

"They all happened working on the case, Perry, darling."

"Mr. Parker, you will admit there's not much in the way of information there." Miss Collins had once again taken on her employer to servant tone.

"Oh, I has some of dat too, Missy Collins," I drawled.

"Well, sir, impart it, this minute."

"Perry, keep your shirt on. Not that you'll ever have to worry about losing it in the market will you? Neither will old T.M." All bets were off now. The damn nerve of this thief of millions accusing me of nickel and diming a client.

"What on earth are you saying?" he asked like a man hoping for a different answer than the one he expected.

"I'm saying, and perhaps a bit too plain and simple for your elegant sensibilities to comprehend, that you and T.M. Collins are both involved in insider trading. I'm not sure yet if that's why T.M. was kidnapped, but I do have the proof that you're both involved."

"Mr. Parker, this was not to be part of your investigation." J.E. could reproof with the best of them.

"And why, Miss Collins, am I not surprised that you seem to have full and prior knowledge of this information."

"Because, Mr. Parker, you were correct when you said you were not the poor, hapless sap I thought you were. But believe me, insider trading, though illegal, is done by practically everyone, everyday on Wall Street and therefore not much of a motive for kidnapping."

I hated her coolness.

"Maybe if I believe you about that, I should also believe you know what the motive is."

"Someone who wants a million dollars, I would suspect."

"Or someone who wants you." I shot a look at Mason. He caught on quickly and didn't like the idea just as fast.

"Janet, tell this oaf to stop with his libelous innuendo at once!"

"I don't know, Perry, you didn't deny the insider pitch and you certainly didn't deny your feelings for J.E. You're a lawyer, help me out on this one, I always get mixed up, which one's libel and which one's slander?"

"Any relationship I may, or may not have with Miss Collins is certainly none of your concern."

"There's where you're wrong, Perry, darling. Anything to do with this case is my concern. And right now you appear to be smack-dab in the middle of everything going on. Why is that?"

"I can account for my whereabouts the entire evening that T.M. failed to come home." His voice was full of confidence and smugness and he managed to get both J.E. and me in his wide sweeping view.

"Mason, do you honestly think that I'd believe you'd have the guts, or stupidity to grab T.M. in person? No. You're definitely a hire-someone-to-do-the-dirty-work-for-you kind of guy."

"Mr. Parker, are you getting anywhere on this case? Time is of the essence, you know?"

"Yes, J.E., I'm well aware of that. And I believe I'm getting somewhere, though to be honest, I'm not all that sure where."

"Then why do you believe you're getting somewhere?"

"That hospital bill you'll be getting. It's for a very good friend of mine who was asking a lot of questions regarding this case. Those questions, I believe, are what got him shot."

"You believe! You believe. Are you sure of anything, Parker?"

I got up and gave him a right hook. He went down. I smiled.

"I'm sure your jaw's as weak as a playboy's alibi, Perry, darling," I said in the general direction of his prone body as I walked back to retrieve what was left of my sandwich from the table. Feeling damn good about myself, remembering that Cudge had informed me that gusseteer was a word used in England just prior to the 1800s and it meant a whoremonger.

He tried to get back up but his legs were anesthetized. J.E. seemed positively shocked by what had happened and as a result, I'm afraid, wasn't lending much assistance. My bet was Mason was going to have to wait until his head cleared and he was able to pull himself together before he'd be able to get back up. It either hadn't occurred to J.E. to call Charles away from the car, or she was reluctant to do so because of the reputation of the neighborhood. Either way was fine with me.

I sat down with my sandwich and offered some to J.E. What the hell, she had given me that gooey custard filled square bun and a cup of tea.

Mrs. Geetus, who could hear a pin drop three houses away, came from nowhere and saw Mason on the floor. "Mr. Parker, you haven't shot another one have you?"

"No, Mrs. Geetus, just smacked him around a bit's all."

"Okay, then. Just see that you don't shoot him." She was being very firm on the point.

"I won't, Mrs. Geetus," I said with as much disappointment in my voice as I could muster.

The looks on their faces were beautiful. Their combined wealth could not afford the joy I was feeling. I loved Mrs. Geetus and her wonderful way of getting things mixed up at the perfect times. J.E. sat down. She was positively glaring at me and at the .45 next to my plate. I smiled. An impish little number complete with flashing eyebrows. She now seemed ready to help Perry to his feet. It was a touching scene. The two of them holding onto each other and just kind of backing out with J.E. saying she'd be in touch. I changed from impish smile to maniacal grin and kept it going till they were half way to the car. It just felt right.

I was disappointed that she hadn't brought a note. Mr. Bellem might think he was a forgotten man.

CHAPTER 12

I was feeling so good I hadn't even minded the train ride to the hospital. Cudge's room was nice. Semi-private, the least J. E. could do. He was in the bed furthest from the door and nearest to the window. Even laying in his position he could see the tops of trees in the park next to the hospital. It was just him and one old geezer who went on about "The Big One." The One to end all others. Only it hadn't, of course. He had caught a whiff of mustard gas and constantly spoke about the hell of the trenches and the sting of the barbed wire. He was the perfect roommate for Cudge. The two of them lobbing "important" facts at each other from over their drawn curtains barricades.

Cudge was glad to see me, even before he knew I snuck him a pint of bourbon and a few unsoaked guinea stinkers. I laughed to myself thinking how the old guy would probably start reliving some major gas attack as soon as Cudge lit one up, and could picture the nurses checking every bed pan on the floor for the source of such a foul odor.

"Listen, Harry," he said, "check my place for the bullet. See if Cutter can match it. Tell him I think it was a cop."

"Did you see the guy? Is that the something? Do you remember who it was?" I pictured myself closing the door on Mason's cell.

"That's the something all right, but I didn't glance the face. Just something about the way the guy moved, or something, I'm not really sure, I just got the impression he was cop."

"All roads lead to Mason, don't they, Cudge?" I said with a triumphant grin.

"Not necessarily, Harry." He was certainly less enthusiastic than I was about the possibility of his shooter being a uniformed hired gun.

"Who else would have the kind of juice to use a cop to waste a guy?" I sealed my argument.

"I don't know. But there are people."

"Yeah, name one." I thumbed my voice at him.

"Mr. Morringello or any of his associates." He poked a sharp stick into my good eye.

"Listen," I said getting up and starting to mull his last comment over, "you take care of yourself. I'll try to stop by again tomorrow, I'm going over to see Cutter now."

"Watch out for shooters, Harry," he said with a friend's true concern.

"They better watch out for me," I said and patted my jacket pocket and let loose a .45 caliber smile. He shot one back.

The old man said something about fixing bayonets while holding on to a part of his anatomy that no longer looked like it was meant for piercing anything. I left without saying goodbye to him, concerned a reflexive salute at that moment could do nothing to improve the situation.

I thought about Cudge on my ride to the 83rd. He and I went way back. I was still on the force the first time we met. He was standing outside the house of a guy who had said his final words a few minutes before. My bet was they went something along the lines of, "please," or, "I've got a wife and kids." Whatever they were they apparently weren't as convincing as he had hoped they'd be.

I was the first cop to arrive, which meant that I had to secure the scene and interview any possible witnesses. I had asked Mr. Congelluno what he had seen to which he replied, "A great many things." We had a short, pleasant conversation and he had struck me as a Damon Runyon character who had fallen out of a book and was trying to find his way in the "real" world. When I asked him what he knew about the dead guy he said, "No one gets out of this life alive." Shortly after this conversation we began to meet in Farrell's and I began to get a lot more information than most other street bulls which probably served only to prolong my inevitable departure from the force.

Cutter was still at the lab. Head deep in a book about chemicals and compounds. He didn't hear me come in even though I almost stumbled over some new tooth x-ray gizmo in the corner. He was a man who could be snuck up on very easily I thought.

"Evening, Doc," I said, figuring to startle him half out of his shoes.

"What's up, Harry? How's Cudge?" Nothing. Not a non-experimental movement swayed through him.

"How did you know I had seen Cudge?" I was impressed.

"Easy. You're a loyal man, Harry. And I detected the faint smell of guinea stinkers and antiseptic solutions, as you were coming down the stairs."

"Stinkers were in my pocket. Smelly stuff, some cleanin' broad spilled on my shoe at the hospital. Damn good trick, Doc, and here I thought you weren't even aware of my presence."

"I wish everything was as easy as that, there's still nothing new on who moved the Collins case to the downtown lab, Harry. Though I did enlist the aid of Kaminsky on it. He's the detective in charge so I figured he'd be able to find out if anybody could."

"You didn't tell him it was for me, did ya?"

"Do you see any bruises?" He stood with his arms spread wide as if I could see through his clothing. I knew it was a joke but I was tempted to say something about the oval shaped purple stain under his left breast pocket resembling a rather large contusion, but then he was liable to tell me what it really was and I didn't think I wanted to know.

Instead I said, "And did he give you any of his brilliant theories on why the case shift?"

"Naw. He did say that it bothered him, too, though. He didn't like people inferring that anybody who worked around here, couldn't get the job done. I think he was sort of sticking up for me."

"Damn decent of him, Doc, though I'd bet he was more worried about his own precious reputation than yours. Probably afraid some downtown guy sitting at his desk will be able to solve the case before him. Probably will, too.

"You know, Doc, asking Kaminsky to help you in matters of detection is kind of like asking Hoover how to get out of the Depression."

"He can't be all that bad. He's solved some cases."

"Confessions obtained at the end of a rubber hose do not really solved cases make, Doctor Cutter." His naivete in such matters, especially given his proximity to Kaminsky and his cohorts, never ceased to astonish me.

"You never told me how Cudge was doing?" He had put down whatever it was that was holding his attention and was now facing me fully.

"He'll be fine. That's kinda why I'm here, though, I need your help. He told me he's got this feeling that the guy who shot him was a bull. Said it was the way he moved, or something. Wants you to check the bullet, see if you can match it. Think, when you're finished here, you and me can go over to his place and take a look around for it?"

"Finished now. Let's go." He took off his lab coat, stuck it in his locker and took out his coat and hat. He said, "You know most people say he did this or that like a cop and others, especially cops think they're crazy. There is however sound logic behind why people think like that."

"Really. Why?" Having been a cop who had heard the accusatorial, "He acted just like a cop," once too often myself, I was interested in what this scientific theory was going to be.

"Because most cops, like most all professions, receive the same training. They're taught to do things in a certain manner, trained in the same way, so soldiers advancing in twos, lawyers touching their lapels during dramatic pauses, or cops shooting with both hands on the gun, in feet wide apart stances naturally all look the same doing it."

"Makes sense to me," I half reluctantly said as we got to the street.

Doc's Pontiac wagon was a lot bigger than the old Buick and I couldn't help but hope, as we climbed in, that live bodies were the only kind he transported in it. But you could never be sure with Doc. The wagon hugged the Brooklyn cobblestone like a jaguar in the jungle and Doc always drove at a lawful speed, but I was glad it wasn't too far to Cudge's place just the same. Doc had a thing for a certain radio station that only played show tunes. The Gentleman Is A Dope, Autumn Leaves and How Are Things In Gloccamorra all rattled around the interior of that big Pontiac Six station wagon like we were sitting in the center of Carnegie Hall. I'd been to Carnegie once, in a box no less, with Thelma all decked out by my side. A bonus, thrown in by a very grateful father in a successful case where I had paid some wise guy off not to marry this rich clown's daughter. He could have saved himself a heap of dough by just visiting the guy and seeing him at home with his pretty wife and their three little kiddies. But then, that might have required some personal contact, God forbid. Not to mention that I wouldn't have gotten my salary, plus ten percent of the payoff, plus the ducats to Carnegie, which believe me did a hell of a lot more for Thelma than they did for me. There hadn't been one tune played the entire evening that you could hum along with.

"You got the key, or something?" Doc interrupted my reminiscences with a perfectly logical question as we pulled up in front of Cudge's joint.

"Or something," I said, realizing only with his question I had neglected to ask Cudge for his keys.

We climbed up past the gilt number, letter system till we hit D2. I slid my picks in and tumbled the lock in about twenty seconds. Doc was genuinely impressed.

"How does someone learn these things, Harry?" he said with his hand held to the side of his face adding physical as well as intellectual befuddlement.

"How does someone learn that X many parts of this, coupled with Y many parts of that, means what he's lookin' at under his microscope is cigarette rather than cigar ash, Doc?" I returned the compliment.

He smiled and we slipped on into the apartment. Someone had obviously slipped on in before us, because even Cudge never left the joint looking like this. The sofa cushions, which if I remembered correctly were never much in the fluffy department, were now nothing more than deflated fabric skins surrounded by big white feathers. Doc shot me a glance that had fear showing through it better than a warm, wet stain on a pair of light gray trousers. And it was the first I realized my forty-five was staring into the bedroom almost begging for an intruder to still be on the scene.

We searched for about twenty minutes with Doc figuring trajectories based on where Cudge said he and the shooter had been standing at the time he was shot. Cudge or Doc or my relay of the information or more than likely a combination of all of the above had been off by a little, but not much, and Doc finally found a hole in the living room wall. The previous intruder was smarter than us and had gotten to it first but then he probably knew just where to look. From the looks of it, he had also been equipped with a penknife and our hole was just that.

"Harry, I really think it's time to go." Doc, who had been at more crime scenes than me, seemed uneasy.

"I guess you're right. No sense hanging around, when you've been beaten to the punch."

"Where to now?" We were putting our coats back on and I was getting my picks back out so I could lock the joint back up. No sense in adding to the temptation of a vacant apartment with an unlocked door. Although, I was certain that nobody who knew Cudge, or knew of him, would rob him.

"Just drop me off at my office, Doc. Got some thinking to do." I smiled to myself hearing the double click of the lock's cylinder.

"Staring out the old brown window again, hey, Harry?"

Staring out the old brown window. Cold women and my refrigerator. Either there is a network of spies on Harry Parker's tail, or, and this is probably much more likely, I talk too damned much when I'm drunk.

Doc's humming along with his tunes combined with my attempts at thought kept the conversation to a minimum and before I knew it he had dropped me off in front of Syd's. He'd said he was sorry about not finding the bullet and added that he'd meet me later for a few cold ones over at Farrell's.

I walked in on Sarah in that perfect bending for the Tootsie Rolls on the lowest counter position. Definitely displaying her best side. I actually made a sucking sound through my teeth thinking of an all the women I'd ever known thrown together for that one ecstasy fulfilling, kill Harry Parker sexually explicit evening which I knew at that very moment would be so damned worth it. She looked up and smiled and I walked on back to my office knowing she had caught me, known just what I had been thinking, and loved every minute of it.

My office was shrinking again. Two boxes of water pistols stood closest to my desk. Insult added to injury. Now every damned kid in the neighborhood would be out there playing clear Harry's window of every possible insight just in case he might, by some stroke of dumb luck, be catching on to something. It was then that it hit me. Brilliance was truly simplicity itself. I went out the back door scooped up some dirt from the yard and put it in Sarah's mop pail. I came back inside squeezed off one small shot from each seltzer bottle, not enough to be missed from any one bottle, used my finger as a swizzle stick, and took my mud and flung it from different angles and in different proportions at the inside of the window. Ha! Screw those little marksmen. They'll never wash away another clue now. I sat down, tilted my chair back against the desk, folded my hands on top of my head and stared at my masterpiece.

I took my cigarettes from my inside jacket pocket, shook out a smoke and stared a bit harder.

Another smoke went by. Then a third.

Miss Gringold, my fifth grade art teacher, had once picked up one of my pictures, tsk, tsk, tsked, admonished me about dripping paint down the sides of my desk and told me that I couldn't draw a sky if I had all blue paints. It now seemed that the old biddy may have actually known a thing or two about art after all.

Maybe if I took a water gun and. ...

"Harry, you're busy, or I'm interrupting something?"

"What's on your mind, Syd? I'm in a kind of lull right now." I turned in my chair to face him.

"Cudgel called while you were out. He wants to know if you got lucky with the slug? And if you go by tomorrow could you sneak him some more cigars. The nurses took the one's you brought today."

I laughed. It was probably old Mustard Gas screaming at the top of his ancient frail lungs that the Germans had launched another barrage that brought the nurses down on Cudge.

"Harry, this isn't funny. You shouldn't bring cigars to a hospital. One spark, God forbid, could blow the whole place into Manhattan. They got gasses and what-nots there, Harry, highly explosive."

"Not where Cudge is, Syd, he's not that sick."

"Not that sick? Not that sick! Getting shot is not that sick? Harry, what's sick to you, a limb on the floor, or a missing head maybe?"

"Okay, Syd, no cigars." I stymied a laugh at his descriptive description.

"Harry?"

"Yes?"

"Is it me, or is the window getting darker?"

"No. Looks the same to me, Syd."

As he walked out he looked at the case of seltzer bottles, then at the window, then at me. It was impossible for him to tell, I thought, absolutely imperceptible. I smiled sheepishly. He shook his head and went back to the store.

CHAPTER 13

I put on my hat and coat and walked over to Court Street. A much better location to hail a cab. Mason's office was across the bridge. The bridge was truly a beautiful structure, but God how I hated to venture across its span. I figured it wasn't called the Brooklyn Bridge because Manhattan was the better side. It was a little late in the day but judging from all the time he put in at J.E.'s house I reasoned that Mason had to work sometime.

My point was proven as we neared Mason's office and saw traffic was being diverted, although we couldn't see why. I took out my shield, which I had kept when "terminated" from the N.Y.P.D., you're not supposed to but every cop has a duplicate or "dupe" made for when he retires and regardless of his new status still desires to reap some of the "on job" benefits. I flashed it to a kid who looked like he wouldn't be shaving for a few years but was nonetheless wearing the blues and directing traffic. He threw a finger in the direction I wanted to go and where the rest of the Joe citizens couldn't without fear of a nasty city tow job and gave me the nod. The cabby pulled over and I threw a "thanks" back at Officer Peachfuzz. A few steps later I stood in front of a skyscraper

that held the offices of John "Sellout" Mason. The elevator start-
er asked people where they were going by the name of who they
were seeing in the building, not floor number. With all the offices
that could fit in this behemoth of a building I was certain this guy
could even impress Cudge.

I got off on thirty-two and by the time I had worked my way past
the two massive outer offices and the third bulldog secretary, I was
almost too tired to ask him any questions. Probably just the way a
guy like Mason had things figured. I knew he'd see me though.
I just told Miss Wicked Witch of the North and South to tell Mr.
Mason I had something new on the T.M. Collins case.

Miss Wicked Witch of the West, was the final obstacle and she
hung to her desk like a seasoned trapeze artist. A ton of makeup
and a major power shortage would have brought her all the way
up to just plain ugly, but as she stood, or sat, she was deserving of
all the pity mustered since time began. I tipped my hat, it almost
jumped back in place from fright. She smiled. Things did not
improve. Her dental records may have been able to prove she was
a throw back to something that very much deserved being thrown
back. I politely told her why I was there. By the time she had finished repeating my spiel into the thick mahogany squawk box on
her desk, Perry's doors were opening and he was motioning me in
with a big wave of his arm and an even bigger smile of approval.

"Nice of you to see me on such short notice, John." I drooled
sarcastic politeness.

"Nonsense, Harold. I'd be remiss in my obligations to the
Collins family if I failed to be circumspect to any leads you may
have developed in the case." He matched me verbal parry for parry with a sharp tongue foil.

"Well, I may have exaggerated a tad there, John." I brought the excitement in my voice down to a serious, leaden tone.

"What do you mean?" His perfect white teeth were still beaming brightly, but some of the gleam had been turned down in his eyes.

"I mean I don't exactly have a lead."

"Just what exactly do you have?" He was not happy.

"Something more in the line of a question."

The smile on his face drooped considerably. His teeth were hiding behind fully closed, betrayed lips. I believe he was contemplating asking me to leave in no uncertain terms.

"You know the workings of City Hall and the Police Department," I pressed on undaunted, "I was just wondering, since we've both got the good of the family in mind and all, if you could help me out on something?"

"What is it?" He offered his question slowly and very guarded. He had moved into his courtroom demeanor that easily.

"Who do you think would have the kind of juice it would take to have the forensics portion of a case investigated at another location, say, oh, I don't know, clear across the borough from where the crime was committed?"

"Hmmm. I don't know, but I don't think it would take a very high source. I imagine that it certainly would not be as difficult as you seem to imply. Why, whose case has been moved and why do you think it's important?"

"Just a couple of murder victims from Sterling Place. I'm just trying to keep things straight in my mind. It seemed a little odd to me is all."

He didn't flinch. Either he didn't connect Ruby and Phil as the case that I was referring to, or he was a better actor than a lot of guys pulling down big bucks on the opposite coast. Of course, I had to keep in mind the fact that he was a lawyer, which not only made him automatic sleaze, it also meant he was used to not tipping his hand.

"I'm sure it happens all the time," he said. "Probably cases going in the other direction as well. But shouldn't you be concentrating your efforts on Miss Collins' case?"

"Oh, I am. I am. This was just a question for a friend, but it's funny though, I'm told it doesn't happen nearly as often as you think, in fact it hardly ever happens."

"More than likely some nervous nelly lab technician giving you bad information," he declared incidentally.

"No. A cop I know fed me the line, but, as you say, you probably have more experience in these matters. Well, thanks for your help and I'm sure I'll be seeing you around."

"Is that all you came for? You could have telephoned with that question."

"Yes. ... " I had to think on my feet, not expecting the question, "but I always wanted to see where the other half worked anyway, as they say, I was in the neighborhood. Very beautiful office you have here." He smiled, accepting my compliment and my story.

His pride in his elegant surroundings obliterating his logic to see past my feeble ruse.

As I walked out past the click-clacking typewriters and the low phone voice mumbling of the three wicked sisters I thought of Mason's last question and my real reason for coming. I figured it would be considered bad form if I told him the real reason for my showing up was that when I ask a guy like him questions, a guy I don't trust, I like to be looking him in the eyes at the time, just in case some of the lie shows up there. It didn't with Mason. Which didn't prove anything by me.

I was also fairly confident that I had deflected Doc's involvement by telling him that a cop had clued me to the case switch, nevertheless I would warn Doc about Mason's suspicious remark when I saw him later at Farrell's.

I walked to the nearest phone booth, dropped a nickel in the slot and gave Skinny Vinny a ring.

"Worse than I thought," he mumbled with a smile on his face that I could read through the receiver. Somehow, it was always worse than he thought.

"Radiator's shot. Ha, I mean shot as in can't be fixed not as in bang, bang. You already knew that."

"You're a riot, Vinny. How much?"

"Well, you got ya one to the radiator, ya one to the carburetor and ya one in the gas line. ... "

"Money, Vinny. Greenbacks. Dead Presidents. How many?"

"Could go as high as a bill, Harry."

"A hundred, for that car? Find other means of sending your kids to Sacred Heart. Harry Parker's tapped out."

"Eighty-five. And that's the best I can do, Harry, on my mother's grave."

"Your mother's alive and in the Bronx, Vinny, in a retirement home. I'm probably paying for that too."

"Seventy-five. Rock bottom, Harry, and only 'cause it's you."

"You're a sweetheart, Vinny, a regular prince. I don't know how you survive with the discounts you give. Though you've probably managed to hold on to that bundle you stashed from all those ration coupons you dealt in while all the boys were over there."

"Low blow, Harry. Don't remember you ever refusing any."

"Seventy bucks, Vinny. Take it or leave it."

"Done deal, Harry. Be ready tomorrow."

I hung up, hating my bringing up the gas ration angle, and the fact that he was right about my taking full advantage of it.

The dull ache in my head, left by Riles' sap, snuck up on me in a soft, courteous throbbing sort of way that seemed to coincide with a breeze coming off the Manhattan side of the Hudson. Laying down was not a plan that seemed out of the question. Getting home, might be. I called Doc Cutter and asked for a lift. He was there in about twenty-five minutes, damn quick for the time of day and his respect for speed limits, which I suspect had seen an exception due to my rather blabbering phone call. Even the show tunes echoing in the big Pontiac were a welcome sound. My ribs were starting to settle back into place and I was glad that Doc's big wagon didn't bounce me around much on the ride home. Over the years I've learned a strange thing about pain, and that is that it can sometimes increase hours after its been inflicted and unfortunately, I am what is considered somewhat of an expert on the subject.

Cutter helped me up to my room and said he'd drop in on me later. I slowly pulled the stuffed chair toward the window, sat down and struggled to get my feet up on the sill. The big clock down the street was going in and out of focus and before I conked out I saw everyone, from John "Perry" Mason to Honest Abe Lincoln, to a beautiful, slightly younger Thelma laughing at me in its face.

J.E. Collins', beauty swam round and round in the dark whirlpool of my subconscious, images of her full red lips and flushed cheeks flitted in and out of focus like a barracuda eating away at my thoughts until my eyes opened to a darker blackness than the nightmare of her devourment.

Night had filled the room and my head was pounding with the exuberance of a bass drum in the Mardi Gras parade. It was ten after eight, official Gold Medal time. I put my legs down and tested to see if they could hold my weight.

"Harry?" I heard Cutter's concerned sounding voice from the other side of the door.

"Come in, Doc, I'm decent, well, I'm dressed anyway." I was standing in a half crouched position, less distance to fall if my legs could not hold me.

The door opened and he looked a little worried from what I could see of him in the dim light from the hall. He threw the switch and almost blinded me in forty watt bare bulb brilliance.

"I've been knocking and knocking. How long you been out?"

"Since right after you left, I guess." My hat was on the floor by the window, but other than that I was still dressed, coat and all, as Doc had left me.

"Maybe you should see Doc Dearborn. You might have a concussion, Harry."

"Naw, I'll be all right. I wouldn't even have a headache if Kaminsky had worked me over, the damn pansy. But Riles hits like a man who hates the world and enjoys showing it. By the way, Doc, thanks for that picture line. What made you think of it?"

"Heard a lawyer in one of the interrogation rooms use it once. Sergeant Delvecchio spit his coffee halfway across the room and practically gave the suspect cab fare to get the hell out of there."

"Well, I'm glad you have a good memory. Probably saved me some teeth and a few more lumps at least. And while we're on this subject, I could swear I heard Riles lock that door behind me, yet you just strolled on in. How is that, Doc?"

"Worst locks I ever saw, Harry, throughout that whole damned precinct. One little key unlocks every one of them."

He held up a small skeleton key and smiled. I joined him, I think. I wasn't sure what body parts were and were not functioning at the moment. Numbness can lie to you that way, but it can also save you a great deal of pain.

"Say, Doc, I forgot to tell you before, but when I asked Mason about the lab switch he more than hinted that he thought a lab technician was feeding me information. Just seems more and more like he's our man."

"I'd be the first to admit I'm not the smartest guy in the world but you were talking to him about work performed in a lab, why wouldn't he think a lab guy fed it to you? I think you're trying too hard to pin it on him."

"Could be, but it's only because the pin sticks so well."

"Sounds a little like Kaminsky logic to me, Harry."

He had me cold there. Maybe if I were Riles I'd start going to work on Mason and have him singing by noon for everything from T.M.'s kidnapping and insider trading to swearing he was in on the Lindbergh baby snatch. I had the feeling that once you got him out of his rich boy protected setting he'd fold like an accordion.

"You sure you're all right, Harry? You look a bit wobbly." He was closer to me now, looking at my eyes, which I think were looking back.

"Just got to get my sea legs." I tried to reassure him.

"We're on dry land," he reminded me.

"Maybe you are, Doc, but I'm rocking like a cabin boy in his first squall."

"Hey, what's this on the floor?"

"I don't know, Doc, but I'd lay you five to one it's in an embossed envelope."

"You're good, Harry," he said as he picked it up and felt the raised lettering.

"I'll give you the same odds there's only five words on that very expensive piece of paper you're looking at."

"Go on. How could you. ... ?" He broke off, looked from the paper to me and back again. Then read aloud, "What are you up to"

He shoved me the note. "It's a mistake," I told him. "It's meant for the boarder down the hall. Someone keeps slipping notes meant for him under my door." I asked him to do me a favor and shove it under Bellem's door. He returned as I was trying to fit my size seven and a half hat on to my now size eight and a half head.

"Let's stop by my office, Doc, I want to check in with Syd before we see where to next."

CHAPTER 14

I t was the longest walk around the corner I'd ever taken. Syd looked up from behind the counter, shook his head and came around to help Doc get me seated on a stool. He handed me three messages from Cudge who must have been keeping the pay phone at the hospital tied up all day. He was the only person I ever knew who welcomed the ring of the phone. I looked down at the first message, which informed me that Steve Taylor had in fact not had a case in fourteen months. And that the last one he worked on was a simple peeper job with both husband and wife now happily remarried and living in Rhode Island and Texas respectively. Not exactly what anyone would classify as a life threatening investigation.

The second message was that Thelma was worried. She had called my place most of the afternoon and had been told by Mrs. Geetus that I could not be disturbed. She had even come over but was met with a greater determination than her own. I took that to mean that Mrs. Geetus, woman of granite will, had, in her rather unceremonious custom, barred Thelma's entry. She had then called on Cudge at the hospital to see if he had heard from me. It was nice to know Thelma was worried, even though I knew she was worried more about her own neck than mine.

The third message, and he actually used a nickel and a trip up the hospital hall on this, was that the Empire State Building took seven million hours of labor to complete. I pictured him smiling in the hallway, bare ass sticking out the back of one of those ridiculous gowns, designed only for women more than likely by some pink powder puff who wished he was one, nurses and visitors alike knowing more of Cudge than I'd ever care to.

Syd looked up at me from behind the counter. When we were both standing he was a good six to eight inches shorter than me even though he walked around on wooden slats back there. He put them down, he said, because it helped his always sore feet, "To walk on the springy wood rather than the cement floor all day."

"Seven million hours of labor," he said in amazement. "Harry, they could have owned their own business for that already."

"Yeah, Syd, and written off half their taxes the way you do."

"Harry," he said and looked at Cutter, "don't be funny in front of Doc, here, he may believe you're serious. He maybe doesn't know your humor like I do. He's a joker, Doc, our Harry. You know that, don't you?"

"Syd, give Doc here a Coke and a coupla cartons of Old Gold's while I give Thelma a ring and let her know I'm still on the case and subsequently, alive."

I figured as long as J. E was paying I might as well throw some business Syd's way. And Doc was now surely a legitimate business expense being not only a provider of information but a part time chauffeur as well, so two cartons of cigarettes were not an exorbitant expenditure for J.E to absorb. Syd didn't wait for me to say a couple of cartons twice, he was on his way down to the other end of the counter before I had taken my first step, with a "Couple of cartons, you betcha," coming out loud and clear.

I hit my booth and dialed her number. The one I'd known but avoided dialing for so long. I had a quick uneasy feeling of Steve answering, then remembered why I was calling and felt better. She answered on the second ring and I could hear the anxiety in her voice. Don't ask me how "Hello" can sound like anything but "Hello," but it did. Maybe it takes a few years of living with someone. Maybe just blind, crazy love, I don't know. All I know is there was an edge there, an edge so steep I wouldn't want to fall off it. She said hello again and added "Harry?" with a softness I hadn't heard in a million years and I remembered moonlit nights, and bathing suits on warm beaches and a walk down the aisle that promised it would last until death itself.

And I said, "Yeah" in the voice of somebody else's broken dream.

She said, "Thank God. Glad you're all right." She continued to talk but the softness and the moment were gone and I knew in that instant that she was just another client and I was just help, hired to get a job done.

I asked her if she had told anyone about the gun, anyone at all.

"What do you take me for, some kind of sap?" she snarled.

"Listen, I'm tryin' to help you is all. You say you didn't shoot Steve. Okay, I believe you. You say he didn't have any cases working.

141

I believe you again. So what does that leave us? Either some guy breaks in, Steve knows where the gun is, goes for it, and the guy beats him to it, which we'll both have to concede isn't very likely, the shape he was in and all. Or," I intoned, "the other guy knows where the gun is to begin with and goes straight for it. Maybe he even knows Steve, since there doesn't seem to have been a struggle."

"You always were pretty good figuring the angles. Got any ideas on who this other guy is?" A trace of hope had appeared in her voice.

"Not yet, but I'd bet it's someone with an axe to grind with you."

"Me? Why?" She was genuinely surprised.

"You've been set up for it too neatly for it to be anything else."

"I can't think of anybody who hates me that much, unless of course you'd wish to confess?"

"No, Thelma, not me. Though I will admit the idea of murder crossed my mind more than once. Except in my scenario Steve wound up taking the rap."

Her silence echoed across the couple of miles of telephone wire as deep as the transatlantic cable itself. Perhaps there was still a cord there to be pulled, I allowed myself an illusion.

I saw Doc pacing back and forth through the glass doors of the booth and knew he had lost interest in whatever Syd was saying, and as the operator droned for another nickel, I realized it was an epidemic and told Thelma I'd call her when I had something.

Doc looked as if he'd cast a ballot for me for just about anything I'd chose to run for as he saw me coming out of the booth.

"Harry, how's Thelma? How's. ... ?" he began in very fast patter.

"Let's go back to my office, Doc." I saved him from begging. Some people just have trouble adjusting to Syd's wild exuberance for things sweet.

"Harry," he said and looked around to make sure Syd hadn't followed us in, "the man's insane. How does he think he can corner the market on a particular treat from a little hole in the wall candy store on the wrong side of Brooklyn?"

"He doesn't really think he can corner the market. He just wants to be there first with something. He figures he'll get the kids coming here on a steady basis if he's the first and only one, at least for awhile, with something new's all."

"I don't know, he sounds like a man possessed." His head was swirling for all it was worth, checking in all directions, to make sure the "Mad Candy Man of Brooklyn" wasn't sneaking up on him, ready to force feed him pounds of chocolate so sweet he'd die of an instant sugar overload.

"He's okay, Doc. He's just got a dream's all. That doesn't hurt, you know."

"Speaking of dreams, or rather nightmares, what the heck happened to your window?"

"What? What's wrong with the window?"

"Looks like some three year old went mud painting with a shovel."

Everybody's a critic. I turned to face the window. I gave it a good stare. Still nobody there. Jeeze, that damn Miss Gringold knew her stuff.

"Harry, it's your day for calls," Syd said over Doc's shoulder, making him flinch, "That rich one from 'The Heights,' with the attitude."

"Thanks, Syd, be right there. Be back in a minute, Doc."

I walked through the little cramped hall that J. E.'s dress had managed to look so ridiculous in and out to my booth. At least she didn't send another note, I thought.

"Good evening, Mr. Parker," she said, chilling the receiver in my hand and mentholating my desires with four quick, cold words.

"Good evening, Miss Collins," I said, trying, but failing, to replicate the ice age in her voice.

"Have you learned anything new"

I was wrong, it was another note. She was just delivering it telephonically. Mr. Bellem will be so disappointed.

"Miss Collins, why is it that an intelligent woman like yourself cannot grasp the simple concept that I will call you when I have something important enough to report?"

"Mr. Parker, why is it that a man as ... well, why can't you understand that you are working for me?"

"Remember way back to when you first 'engaged' me and you said you don't know how to go about this? Well, let's assume you were correct, you don't. But I do. So let me go about this in my way, which doesn't include so many notes and phone calls, okay?"

"Not really, but I suppose at this late date I'm stuck with you." The receiver froze in my hand.

"Nice to know you still have such unwavering confidence in my abilities, J.E. Goodbye."

I hung up and walked back to Doc. He was sitting in my chair, staring at the window, shaking his head and muttering tsk, tsk, tsk. I wondered if he was related to Miss Gringold, then remembered his lab smock and realized he couldn't be.

"See anything interesting, Doc?"

"What possessed you to throw dirt on the inside of your window. You even dripped it down onto the walls."

Well, maybe he was a distant cousin.

"Hey, Doc, who were the last guys Size Eleven and The Brain worked with?" I asked changing the subject.

"Why?"

"Well, Size Eleven is with Ruby and Phil when they die and at the Collins place repairing refrigerators and installing bugs. We don't know who he was working for but maybe, just maybe, tailing who he was last working with will help us find out. It could be that more than just the two of them and their boss were involved."

"A long shot, Harry." He went to the window, touched the dried mud and turned to look at me.

"All we've got right now. Think you can find out who it was?" I lit a smoke and looked at my desk.

"Levine and Delvecchio. Found out when I was asking about Rogers and DeLuca."

"You know what shift they're on?"

"Graveyard. Volunteered for it."

"Interesting. Well, it's about nine now, we have plenty of time to get to the 83rd, want to speak to Syd some more or hit Farrell's?"

"Don't kid with me, Harry. Joe, the bartender, working on his fifth girlfriend this month has much sweeter stories than Syd."

"Yeah, thinkin' about Angie makes my mouth water more than a Milky Way does too."

"You're a bit behind the times, Harry, Angie was last week. This week's Rita, Angie's younger, and prettier sister."

"I didn't know there was anyone younger and prettier than Angie, not anyone legal anyway."

"With Joe, who knows if they're legal." He shrugged.

"Well, he meets them at the bar doesn't he?"

We walked out past the Wise potato chip boxes and the Wise old owl was winking at me. So, I could swear, was Doc.

A young couple, kids of about thirteen, were sitting at Syd's counter drinking chocolate shakes through straws.

"That's what I like about you, Tommy," the girl was saying, "you're not like the other boys. They're all so jejune."

I had to fight back a smile. Either I was getting older, or jejune had taken on new meaning, 'cause Tommy looked to me to be the very definition of jejune. Then again maybe using the word jejune is the very definition of the word.

"Thanks, Sheila," he said, with a sheepish grin. "I think you're swell too.

The English language had nothing on old world traveler Tommy, all right.

Syd was beaming. Not that he was such a great romantic or ardent admirer of young love or anything even remotely like that. He just knew that two teens in love could spend more on chocolate shakes, while trapped in that great emotional pull of never wanting to say goodnight, better than any other kind of customer he had. He pushed the Wise potato chip rack a little closer to them. Tommy offered Sheila a bag. The salted thirst smile on Syd's face grew dangerously closer to his ears.

Doc's and my reflections grew larger in the darkness of Syd's front window as we got closer to the door. I turned and tapped Tommy on the shoulder and said, "Now you kids have a nice evening."

"Thanks, Mister," they answered as one, proving the future Mr. and Mrs. possibilities of their already blooming relationship. Tommy ordered two more shakes and by the time Doc and I hit the door Syd was enthusiastically whistling a merry little tune that I'd just bet Doc could name in three notes.

CHAPTER 15

D oc's wagon was right outside the door so the rain coming down in sheets was only a minor inconvenience. Those show tunes were more to be worried about. The big Pontiac was a fine piece of machinery, heavy and strong, gliding easily over the streets as the motor purred low, humming almost as habitually as J.E.s' cat. Doc stopped at all the reds and moved his head in time to the music or the wipers or both. An unsuspecting drunk darted out from between parked cars but he didn't catch Doc asleep at the wheel. He swerved and braked only inches from the souse who pulled back in surprise, then staggered away and shouted a "Fuck you" from the safety of the opposite sidewalk. Doc returned the Brooklyn obligatory, "Tell it walkin'" out his quickly opened window.

We were on the bridge over the Gowanus Canal when I got a funny feeling. The Gowanus was a place that gave you a funny feeling at high noon, no less in the pitch black of a rainy night. It was where a lot of wise guys wound up if they got a little too wise. There were probably more wreaths thrown into that shallow bit of water than at Pearl Harbor.

By the time we pulled up to Farrell's the feeling was gone. There was a big, inviting spot right in front of the joint. Doc, being smarter than me, or maybe just remembering what had happened to the Buick, pulled around the corner onto the side street to park. As we walked back we saw a shadow leaning back against the wall, fixed in an almost perfect vanishing point.

"Hey, you the bum workin' the Collins caper?" the shadow whispered through gritted teeth.

"What's it to ya?" I politely snarled back.

"Friend a mine says I should help ya. Don't know's I should now I heard your attitude."

"Gee, pal, I'm so sorry I hurt your feelings. I didn't know they were so delicate. This friend of yours have a name or do I just take your word someone sent ya?" I tried peering into the darkness but even the moon was being too lazy to help and I couldn't make out anything past the voice.

"Cudgel. Give me a call from the hospital. Says you're all right, I should give ya a hand till he gets out."

"Good old Cudge," Doc threw in. "Harry here visited him you know."

"Yeah, I heard. He got tossed of them cigars, ya know."

"Yeah, I heard. Did they find the drink?"

"Naw. He hid the bottle in the General's bed pan. Lucky the old guy didn't get a little more scared, if ya catch my drift."

"I'm drifting with you. What's your name?" I eased out at him.

"What's in a name, friend. All ya gotta know is I'm here to help." He was still hidden in shadow but I could feel the expression changing on his face.

"Well, you do know our names." Doc was helping me again.

"Ain't exactly so, pal. Him I know. Fits Cudgel's description down to the worn out topper. You, were not part of the package ... described."

He stepped away from the wall and into the glow of the street light. I felt positively handsome. He even made Charles look good. Unfortunately, he also made him look small. His face was gaunt and full of the kind of acne parents preach to their kids about if they see them squeezing pimples. The deep scarred kind that never go away no matter how old you get. The blotches couldn't even decide on a color. There were reds and browns with a purple here and there for bad measure. The centerpiece of this tormented piece of inhumanity was a veined blue/red nose that could put the worst drinkers to shame.

Still, it was hard to miss his size through it all which I guess in his case was an asset. It was also probably why Doc blurted out, "Just how the hell big are you, anyway?"

"Six-foot-seven," he beamed, pride in every inch. And somehow just hearing the size made him look an inch or two taller and uglier.

"Tell me, friend," I said, "just how is it you can help me?"

"Same as Cudgel, only I ask a fair price for my services."

"By fair I take it you mean more." I twisted my face a bit, trying to match the ugliness of increased costs for the same services rendered.

"I mean fair for what you need to know and for what I can deliver." He was damn sure that he knew exactly what I wanted.

"And suppose we don't agree on fair?"

"Then I stop helpin'. No hard feelings, no monies owed, I just walk away."

"Well, now that sounds ... fair, Harry." Doc was just bubbling over with jubilant assistance tonight.

"And since I don't know your name, how do I get in touch with you?" I inquired reasonably.

"You don't. You tell me what you need and I get you when I get it. I got Syd's number, and Geetus', and, of course, here." He threw a thumb back at Farrell's. It was sad to realize, but he had my life's habits pretty well covered in three small pieces of real estate.

"I thought Cudge was getting sprung from the hospital?" I said with the proper amount of annoyance in my voice to match the occasion.

"Naw, some kind of infection or something, be there another few days or so. You got that long?" He answered with, - he had me there and he knew it - proper reflection.

"Okay, pal, let's give you a try. Where did Miss Collins get my name for starters and what kind of action is this Mason guy in on down on Wall Street? Think that will hold you for a while?"

"Doesn't sound like much, I'll be callin' you at one of these places as soon as I have something. You be ready to pay, chum."

He slithered down the avenue and even at his height faded into the darkness like the Shadow with the ability to cloud men's minds to the point of believing that he was invisible.

Doc and I went into Farrell's. Joe was talking up three dames at once. Each properly distanced at the bar so none could hear Joe's patter when he was with one of the others. And each was artfully being persuaded that all other women at the bar were "mere customers who paled in their beauty, charm and intelligence when compared to her." I actually heard him say this to the dame standing next to me at the time. So I knew it would be quite a while before he got around to taking our order. I reached over the bar and grabbed a few long necks. With the peripheral vision of an eagle and the agility of a leopard, Joe spun on his heels with the Brooklyn weapon of choice, a Louisville Slugger, in his hands. He saw it was me and smiled. "Harry, help yourself, just do me a favor and keep score, will ya?"

I guess all that paying up of your tabs every time you get a few bucks pays off in the, "He's an honest guy," department. Most of the slobs at the bar seemed properly impressed by my preferred customer treatment and I soaked it in on my way over to the table.

We were working on our third beer, sitting at one of the smaller tables in the back of the joint, and I was watching Joe at work. "Joe really knows how to give them all the time of day," I said, filling in some conversation.

"Yeah, and then something much more penetrating," Doc shot out. I gave him a surprised look, but he didn't look up from his Rheingold label. About a half a minute later he unexpectedly came out with, "You know, Harry, I am a doctor. I don't practice medicine, not on live people mind you, but I am a doctor nonetheless."

"That's nice, Doc, I always figured you were."

"What I mean is, if we were to go over to Brooklyn Hospital, even at this late hour, and you were to, say, introduce me as Doctor Cutter, Mr. Congelluno's personal physician, I'm quite sure we'd be able to get in to see him."

My smile was big and broad but didn't equal the respect I had for the man who sat across from me, obviously reading my mind.

"You mean you don't exactly trust this nameless shadow laden with good intentions either, huh, Doc?"

"That about sums it up. I'd like to hear Cudge say he sent the guy and I'd feel a whole hell of a lot better if he told us the guy's name and where we could get in touch with him."

"Our wave lengths sure are clicking tonight, Doc. Only we'll need some medical garb."

"Let's stop off at my lab and get my smock. It looks enough like a doctor's hospital jacket, especially at this hour of the morning."

I shot him a not so discrete gander.

"I do have a clean smock, Harry." He was really getting very good at anticipating what I was going to say.

We hit the men's room then headed for the car after I dropped some cash on the bar and gave Joe a wave he never noticed. I can't say I blamed him. She was of that girlish/womanish age when the softness and firmness are still in the right places. She passed him a round coaster and from the easy way he pocketed it, I knew her phone number and probably more personal information was on it. Joe must have had more coasters at home than at work. It was a rare event when he would use one for something as trivial as a buffer between wet glass and dry bar.

The wind had picked up and even the short walk to Doc's wagon was a cold one.

Old Devil Moon was coming from the radio as we waited for the engine to warm sufficiently before Doc would put her into gear. I pulled out the dashboard lighter, watched the little red glow light the end of my cigarette and looked out the window to check the moon. It looked about the same as it always did. Maybe a little less full, a little duller, but not particularly Devilish.

CHAPTER 16

A doctor who looked like it would be a while before he was old enough to get his drivers license was wrapping bandages around the wrists of a young girl who had done her damnedest not to get any older. She sobbed in a very low voice about the boyfriend who had gotten her in this "condition" and then walked out on her. It was impossible to tell if she was crying for him, for her condition, or for the fact that she had failed in her attempt to show him how much he'd really miss her. A nurse was sticking a needle into the massive backside of a guy who screamed like a baby, calling her a butcher and a few other choice names that were usually associated with a profession even older than nursing. Other people sat waiting, heads hung, blood seeping through badly improvised bandages, silent or moaning. None of them noticed us as we walked through the hectic Emergency Room and up the stairs to the right. Doc, in his smock, carrying a clipboard he had taken from his lab, mumbled some medical-sounding gobbledygook to me about my Cousin Tony as we breezed through. The clipboard was a nice touch. I wasn't sure about the gobbledygook, maybe it was actual medical terminology, maybe it was pure gibberish that another doctor could hear right through. Whatever it was it didn't make any difference because no one but me heard it anyway.

We heard a voice from the room and wondered who Cudge had cornered at this hour of the night, but as we tiptoed in we realized that both patients were fast asleep and the General was merely reliving some long ago fought battle. Doc took some Guinea stinkers from his pocket and waved them under Cudge's nose. After all, I had promised Syd I wouldn't bring them, and I didn't. Cudge woke up smiling and asked for a match. I suggested that they could keep until after our talk, just in case they had the same effect that they had the last time.

"Of course I'm sure, Harry," Cudge was grousing after hearing my description of the evening's events, "it's not exactly the kind of thing I'd forget. I didn't take the bullet in the head, ya know. I'm tellin' ya, I never sent anyone, nameless or otherwise, to help you out. You know I work alone. You know that too, right, Doc?"

"Right, Cudge."

"And a guy six-foot-seven I'm not about to easily forget here, Harry." He was getting a little too excited and a lot too loud.

"Calm down, will ya, Cudge. We believe ya. Why do you think we came here at this hour of the night? The whole damn thing sounded screwy to us, too. Right, Doc?"

"Right, Harry."

"I'll make a few calls and find out who this joker is, Harry. Then when I get out I'll have a little friendly chat with him myself. Just sort of let him know it ain't nice to use a guy's name when he don't know you're usin' it, see. I got a reputation to protect here, ya know?" He threw the covers back and started to get up forgetting all about the liquidy goo dripping into his left arm.

"Hold on, pal," I said as I put my hand on his chest. "It's a little late for phone calls and besides you need your rest."

"I need my rep more than sleep right now, and that means finding out who this bum is."

"I know that, but I'd appreciate it if you'd do me a favor and don't noise anything about this guy around just yet. I'd like to see what he brings me on Collins and Mason before he has a chance to catch wise that we're on to him."

"Okay, Harry, for you. But when it comes time to dealin' with him, I'm the dealer."

"You got it, Cudge. Croupier to the six-foot-seven crowd sounds more up your back alley than mine anyway." I gave him my best he's-all-yours nod.

"Guy takes a few lousy days off the streets and right away some bum figures he can start tossin' his name around. Ain't right, Harry. Ain't right at all."

I handed him his lighter as we were leaving figuring a smoke might help calm him down. It had been on the floor of his apartment and I didn't want any fires starting because of it. Doc shot me a look. "I never promised Syd I wouldn't give him a light." I offered in defense of his reproachful gander.

Doc's look softened to a lopsided grin as we walked down the stairs together. The kid doctor was at work on an even younger kid's head. A needle and thread moved in and out as if he were a seamstress pulling together the crazy quilt pattern of the kid's life.

"Not bad," Doc whispered to me, as we both paused and stared at the professional craftsman at work.

"He's as good at putting them together as old Finkelstein, the medical examiner, is at taking them apart," Doc said with the admiration in his voice reaching across the small space between the two of us and touching me with the warmth of its sincerity. I took another look around the big room and realized just what a tough night the kid doctor was in for.

We got in the wagon and Doc repeated his warm up ritual. The radio was giving us the weather. It told us it was cold. Which was one of the few things that we already knew.

It was a slow, quiet ride with the rain turning to a light snow just beginning to fall. Charles was sitting on my stoop, a couple of sheets of newspaper separating his backside from the thin coat of snow on the unshoveled steps as we pulled up behind the huge, highly polished Collins limousine. Even with just the light from the lamppost across the street I could see he had an envelope in his hand and a scowl on his face. He looked like he was up way past his bedtime and not enjoying it one bit.

"Evening, Charlie boy," I said forgetting my self-reminder to be more polite to the axe murderer.

"Evening my ass, where you been all night when ya shoulda been working on Mr. Collins' case!"

It certainly wasn't phrased in the form of a question and I could clearly see the axe in Charles' eyes.

"We have been working on the case," Doc said, helping again, "just came from a meeting with an informant, if you must know."

"No. I mus'aint," Charles said with a sharpness in his voice that seemed to cut way past anger, "all I must do is deliver this here friggin' note and get back to bed. And don't let me find out you're workin' on this Taylor murder case when you should be working for Mr. C. Here!"

His words came out in one long growl. He stabbed the note at me like a matador's final thrust at the bull.

"Good night," Doc offered to the stone wall walking past him on its way back to a shiny limousine, a short ride and a warm bed.

It went unrejoindered.

I stuck the envelope in my pocket and thanked Doc for driving me around all night.

"Aren't you going to open it?" he said in that same frantic way Thelma used to when I'd put a friend's Christmas present, given on December 18th or there about under the tree not to be opened until Christmas.

"Naw, I think I'll save it to read with my breakfast. It can take the place of the morning paper I never seem to get to anyway."

"What if it's important?" The, "this could be the greatest gift ever" emergency ringing in his voice like a midnight alarm on a quiet street.

"Look, Doc, it's short, it's to the point, it's damned annoying, and it's probably about working harder, or faster, or reporting in more often, but it's not important, believe me. Thanks again, Doc. I really appreciate the cab service."

"But, Harry, how would she know whether or not you're working hard enough?"

"Mason's probably been whispering some very unsweet, he's doing nothings, in her ear would be my bet. Not that it would take much, I don't think one can ever work hard enough when working for a Collins. Good night, again, catch you tomorrow."

"Good night, Harry."

He headed back to the wagon and I felt him watching me from behind the wheel, as I went up the steps. When the door closed behind me he turned over the engine and waited until he thought it was warm enough before he pulled away from the curb with a show tune playing a bit too loud for the time of night.

I had already undressed and thrown myself at the bed, stopping only long enough to pour my morning wake up swig, when I heard a low creak in an old floorboard.

I grabbed the .45 from the nightstand and threw on the light switch at about the same time. He was standing against the far wall. Not that anything was too far away in my small room, but at this hour a six-foot-seven ugly guy seemed very close indeed.

"I woulda thought you was a PJ's man myself." He grinned.

"That's the problem with knowing your own apartment too well," I said, "you get all comfortable, and lazy. You forget the little things, like turning on the light to see if there might be a rat, got into the cheese while you were out."

"Uncalled for, Harry boy. I'm your helper, remember?"

"Oh, yeah, I mustta forgot. But that's only because you make it so easy, standin' in the shadows, breakin' and enterin' and all that."

"Harry, Harry. Look around you. What's broken? You have a door with no lock, and if you take a minute ... maybe thirty seconds, you'll see none of your vast fortune has been tampered with."

"Guess you're right, friend," I decided to see what info, if any, the joker had brought me before getting too upset. Besides, it was my own carelessness, more than the fact that he had let himself in that had gotten my steam up.

"What have you got for me?" I quizzed in a far calmer frame of mind.

"Fifty smackers." He held out his giant paw, which I noticed for the first time possessed the same blemishes as his face only darker and rougher looking.

"Fifty!" I nearly screamed, but remembered Mrs. Geetus. "For fifty I could have my own mother knocked off."

"Your mother's gone. Ten years now, Harry."

That shook me more than finding him in my room. No mere informant is going to waste a paying night looking up trivial information on the life and times of Harry Parker. Not unless he's working both ends against the middle and some other joker's paying him to spy on me, I thought.

"You tell me what you got first and then I see if it's worth it. Remember?"

"John Mason is in 'on the ground floor' as they say, of some kind of new machine. A machine that's going to revolutionize the business world. It's something called a comp utter or something like that. It's a big fancy adding machine and he's not only buying up all he can, he's selling the information about it to some other high rollers. Why? you might ask. Because then he uses that money to buy more of the company. All of this, I needn't say, is very, very illegal, but I'm sure you could have figured that part out on your own."

I just stared at him trying to figure out how much of it was real. The big man saw it as a sign that he hadn't given enough for the price he had asked.

"Okay, that's not the half of it," he continued, "the real news is that T.M. was in on it too, and was trying to stop Mason from selling the information to others. He called him everything from a fool to an effing idiot. And claimed he would stop him 'By any means possible' were the exact words used. Next day T.M.'s as missing as Judge Crater. Now a million's being asked for him. Guess you could buy a lot of that there stock for a million bucks."

I went to my pants pocket, gave him forty, and showed him a lonely fiver in the wallet.

"I'm not holding out on ya," I said, "it's worth the fifty, I'll have the other sawbuck in the morning, as soon as I see the Collins dame."

The big man's mouth curled into something like a smile. It didn't add any pleasantness to his face, but it didn't make it any worse either.

"Oh I trust ya, Harry boy. Cudgel told me you were a man of honor. I'll pick you up somewhere in the day tomorrow and add that ten spot to my treasure chest."

"What about the Collins dame?" I stopped him short of the door.

"What about her?"

"You were supposed to find out why she hired me for the job. Remember?"

"Didn't get that one yet. But I will, Harry. I will." His smile was much broader than before. At least he had good teeth.

So there were some things he couldn't find out, I thought as the door opened and closed and the smell of cheap after shave began to fade. I took the bottle from the drawer and threw down a couple of belts. I put it back, turned off the light, and stared at the darkness, its void roaring back at me. I'll find out who you are, man of shadows, you smug son of a bitch, I thought, just before succumbing to the events of the long day and the alcoholic content consumed.

CHAPTER 17

FRIDAY, JANUARY 10TH

Loud singing interrupted by intermittent coughing and hocking in the hallway woke me from a sound sleep. Mr. Bellem on his way to work again. Older men with sinus conditions should never be permitted to fall in love with younger women. Laws should be passed and strictly enforced. It should be declared an illegal act punishable by banishment to an island inhabited by their honking, phlegm spewing peers. I reached for the drawer, head spinning, eye unfocused and mind oblivious to everything except "Look To The Rainbow" sung very off key by my neighbor on his way to the woman who put stars in his eyes, a song in his heart and very soon another note under his door.

I leaned on my elbow and threw back my bourbon, then just lay there smoking a cigarette and watching the room come into view. The table was still there, so were the chairs and the sink. No new note on the floor, no Mrs. Geetus and no six-foot-seven giant. Okay, inventory over, time to slip on the slippers, the god-damned Thelma-given slippers and shuffle over to my Corn Flakes. Thelma. I had to find out who killed Steve. I can't let her take the fall on this one, especially not to Kaminsky. I wonder if Doc Cutter can get away from the lab today. Maybe he and I can go over Thelma's whole apartment and see if we come up with anything. I know sure as hell if Kaminsky thinks he's got his suspect, and he does, he's not going to go out of his way looking for minor things like clues, or evidence, or actual guilty parties.

I reached for my jacket to get J.E.'s note from last night. I tore open the envelope.

The man's murder must wait

J.E. was getting sloppy. It was a five worder all right but if I didn't figure Mason for still having friends in the D.A.'s office I might not have connected the note to the Taylor murder case. It was just as well I hadn't opened the envelope last night, I really would have had one hell of a time trying to figure this one out in the condition I was in. But, then again, it won't be easy for Bellem either.

The note, like everything else in life, looked softer after I had finished my Corn Flakes. I let it lay on the table as I put my last bowl in the sink. Tomorrow would be dish washing day, hell I might even wash them all. I figured by the time I showered, shaved, dressed and walked over to Vinny's, he'd have the old Buick back in action. Then to see J.E., fill her in on Mason's activities and give an update on fee and expenses.

I was just finishing pulling my tie into a perfect Windsor knot when Mrs. Geetus came in.

"Mr. Parker, these notes really must cease. I am not Mr. Bellem and you are not part of any appointed rounds which I must complete, regardless of rain, sleet, and whatever other nonsense is in that childish credo."

She handed me another J.E. envelope, informed me that she didn't wear black because she was widowed, spun on her heels and left to the sound of my tearing into it. I paused a minute trying to figure out what Mrs. Geetus had just said but gave it up in favor of J.E.'s note.

"I must see you. Now"

I'm starting to get used to it, I thought, but Charles must be fuming with so little sleep. I was impressed. This one contained an actual punctuation mark.

On my walk to Vinny's I passed Mrs. Guerrino, old, walking slowly, arms full of groceries, eyes peeking around brown paper bags that extend over her head. I offered no assistance, she has refused it since my childhood and will continue to until one of us is gone. I tip my hat, she says something in Italian and smiles, deftly side-stepping one of the Thompson kids wildly wheeling his tricycle. We are friends for years, for life, neither ever speaking a word that the other understands, both feeling happier for having known each other.

Vinny is waiting, both hands extended, one with my keys and the other palm up. He looks like he's been shot when I tell him I'll catch him later on the bill. He pauses for a minute, keys dangling in his hand, then, I guess, remembering I'd never stiffed him he lets them drop without any further protestation.

"Sure, Harry," he says, "catch you on the rebound."

I have no stories about blondes and lookalike lovers so the tank does not get a complimentary fill-up. The gas gauge is at the half-way mark which considering the short amount of driving I'd done since I'd picked it up has me looking around for signs of use by young lovers or middle aged businessmen or anyone who'd pay for a '38 Buick as a loaner. There are none. Either I am getting worse mileage than I'd thought, or Vinny is real good at cleaning up after nights before.

I shoot Vinny a look like I know something but he has none of it and goes back to work on a big four door Caddy that he probably wishes he was working on nearer to Prom night.

I headed over to the 83rd and found a spot about two blocks east of the front door. I never parked too close just in case Kaminsky spotted the car and figured I'd be with Cutter. He would give Doc grief for helping me with anything. Bernie was not what you'd call a "hands on" detective. In all the time he'd been on the job I'd bet he'd been to the lab only once or twice. Who needs a lab and clues and evidence and such when you have a rubber hose. But if he spotted my car he would somehow find his way down the stairs.

Doc was in, of course, bent over some smoking beakers that he was adding carefully measured amounts of chemicals to and getting as excited as all hell about the bubbling, boiling troubling results.

He put down what he was working on and looked at me, his hair more frazzled than usual. "I played a hunch," he said. "Recognize these two?"

He handed me standard police mug shots of a much younger Ruby and Phil, or rather of a Sally Mancusso and a Peter Sabatelli. They both had aliases and minor but lengthy rap sheets, but the last couple of words on each card is what Doc knew would catch my eye. Police Informant. I knew that was used to keep small time operators operating so they could pass on information to whoever they were stooling for, either for someone in the department, the Feds, or ... even the D.A.'s office.

"Gee, and we know who could get information from his good pal the D.A. any time he wanted it, don't we Doc?"

"John 'Perry' Mason," Doc answered, now seeming to be more readily accepting of my theory of Mason's complicity.

"I have to see J.E. but I'm glad I stopped by here first. After I've spoken to her you think you can shake yourself loose for a while, I want to toss Thelma's place. I'd be willing to bet it wasn't a priority for Kaminsky and company and I haven't given it a going over yet myself."

"Got lots of sick time, not that anybody would even notice I'm gone."

"Thanks, Doc, I'll spin by when I'm finished over at the Collins place. I got a feeling a certain lady ain't gonna be too happy with her boyfriend, may need a shoulder to cry on."

"Be careful, Harry, she seems more the type to need a back to put a knife in than a shoulder to cry on, to me."

I thought that over on the way to the Buick but shook if off as much happier thoughts of Mason's guilt glided tangos across the highly polished dance floors of my mind.

After only five songs and twice as many advertisements had played themselves out on the radio I was coasting into a parking spot in front of the Collins estate. A very groggy looking Charles answered the door. It took him two rings.

"What's a matter, late night, Charlie boy?" I chirped as I walked on past him and turned back to add "Mistress of the house up yet?"

I was feeling very pleased with myself.

"Don't call me Charlie boy, and don't ever walk in less I say you can. Got it?" Charles was obviously not a morning person and I could tell that he wasn't going to be sharing any of my joy either.

"That will be enough of that, Charles," Miss Collins said firmly from the staircase. Charles turned toward me, I smiled, he sneered back at me, took my hat and reduced it a size or two in his hand, threw it on a gaudy looking table that was more than likely there for the specific purpose of hat holding, and quietly disappeared.

"I'm glad to see you finally took one of my notes seriously, Mr. Parker. Come, let us go into the drawing room."

We sat where we had before, and again tea and cakes had already been placed out.

"I must tell you Mr. Parker that Mr. Mason is growing very weary of your ... shall we say, inactivity, on the case. He has requested, rather strongly, that I dismiss you and allow him to deliver the money to the kidnapper. He is certain that he is a calmer influence, and as such, his presence better insures the safe return of my father. He insists that you are concentrating a disproportionate amount of your time and efforts on another case, one, I believe, involving your ex-wife."

"And you, Miss Collins. What have you decided?"

"That's what I admire about you, Mr. Parker, you don't even take the time to confirm or deny Mr. Mason's allegations. You just press straight ahead with questions of your own."

"You've already made your decision Miss Collins and I like conserving my energy and my breath."

"Quite right, Mr. Parker, and I've decided, although I'm not at all sure why, not to back off my first instinct."

"I'm glad of that, Miss Collins, because I've uncovered some things which might interest you."

"Such as, Mr. Parker?"

"Oh, such as four or five little tidbits that add up to one big conclusion. First, Mr. Mason is very into an insider trading scheme that could be the biggest thing on the market since the crash. Second, your father is in on it too."

"I've already. ... "

"Don't interrupt, J.E. Please."

She pursed her lips and looked as if she were about to ring for Charles, but considered it a second and motioned for me to continue.

"Third, and this is a biggie. Mason was selling the information in order to get more money to pour into the venture on his own.

"Fourth, your father told him, in no uncertain terms, to cease selling the information because too many people were getting in on a good thing."

"That sounds like Father."

"Miss Collins, I am not finished."

"Do continue, by all means, Mr. Parker."

"Fifth, Ruby and Phil, the same Ruby your father was spending so much time with, are both listed among many other things, as police informants. More than mere coincidence, I'm afraid when you consider your father's disappearance coincided so closely with his amorous interests in Ruby. Add to it that Mr. Mason's business dealings and close association with the D.A., which would certainly give him access to police information on informants, probably ties him to the very same Ruby, and. ..."

"Well, well, Mr. Parker, you have been a busy little bee, haven't you?" She looked genuinely impressed with what she had heard if not who she had heard it from.

"Gee, teacher, you mean even without all those book reports I may pass the course?"

"Easy, Harry, Father's not home safe and sound just yet." For the first time since I'd met her I noticed an unrehearsed softness in her voice.

Well, at least I'm back to Harry, I thought.

"No, but we're pretty sure of who's keeping him, if not where he's being kept." I took a bite of creme square bun, without gooing up the works.

"You're pretty sure. You've gathered a lot of information, I'll grant you that, but none of it is any real proof that John is involved. And quite frankly, I don't believe he is."

"Tell me, J.E., just what will it take to convince you of his involvement, a signed confession, or perhaps merely another of your fathers appendages?"

"Now you are being too impertinent, Mr. Parker." She handed me a stack of twenty dollar bills I pocketed without counting and added, "I believe, Mr. Parker you must have a lot to do to prove these accusations before tomorrow midnight." There had been very little time to grow used to that vocal softness.

"Yes, Miss Collins, I'm afraid I really must be going." I took another gooey bun for the road and headed for the hall. "Please don't get up, I can find my own way by now." I threw back over my shoulder at my very seated hostess.

I scooped my hat off the marble table Charles had thrown it on and put it on as I walked across the foyer. Charles walked toward me, I guessed to open the door. He stopped me dead in my tracks by grabbing my arm and stopping the flow of blood to my fingers, "Don't let anything go wrong, Chum," he said, "I got a real sweet set up here."

It was the second time in under five minutes I was wrong about people's reactions. I'd thought J.E. would be happy to know I was onto something that might save her father, even if that something was her boyfriend.

I let the engine run a few minutes, lit up a smoke and looked at the old stone facade that was the Collins ancestral home. Looking at the ornate gargoyle over the door, a calculating madness reflected in its hollow eyes struck me that this latest bit of information was found rather quickly and by a source I wasn't at all sure of. I decided to check in on Cudge before I swung back around to pick up Doc.

I made a quick stop before heading for the hospital and then was on my way. When I entered his room he was squawking about breakfast to the back of a nurse on her way out of his room and not paying much attention to him at all. "How do youse broads expect a guy to get well enough to get the hell outta here on this mush." He was holding his spoon up about ten inches in the air, tilted at a forty-five degree angle, watching something of a yellow liquid consistency slide from it back down onto his plate.

"Calm down, you big lug, you'd think somebody was shooting at you again."

"Harry, look at this slop," he said as he tilted his plate toward me without even a good morning. He was that encouraged at seeing a sympathetic face. The smell alone was enough to kill my appetite but the liquid consistency of what I supposed was meant to be solid food would have stopped a starving man dead in his tracks.

"Cudge, has old Harry ever let you down?"

He gave me a raised eyebrow look, which spoke volumes about what he thought of my reliability.

"Recently, I mean. Past month or so."

Having gotten no better reaction I took the bag with three Whelan's doughnuts from my jacket pocket and waved it around for effect.

"Whelan's," he said, "Harry, you're a life saver."

I let him glom down all three before I said a word. The smile on his face told me my stop had paid off and the grumbling bear was once again his friendly self, ready for conversation.

"Cudge, this big guy, that you didn't send," I began, "he tells me Mason's in on this new machine thing called a comp utter or something. According to him it's something very big, very inside. Think you can get any dope on it?"

"Some professor up at Harvard has something called the Mark I. It's an electromechanical computer. If that or something like it is going public it's very, very big news indeed, Harry. You say this new guy gave you the lowdown, huh?"

I could see the territorial worry on his face.

"Yeah, Cudge, that's why I came to you. No sense trusting the word of an amateur when you got a professional handy." I didn't bring up the fact that I had already imparted this information to my client.

He cheered up a bit.

"Listen, Harry, why don't you get outta here now. I got a lot of calls to make. Get back to me around noon. I'll have more for you by then." He called the nurse, slipped her a five spot, told her to get him two rolls of nickels and keep the change. She started to say something, figured the dollar profit and curbed the indignity from her face and mind and left the room.

I slipped him a fin for the info and forgot to mention the new guy's fee for services rendered. Even though he was in a hospital I didn't see the need to test their cardiac care unit. Besides, if he did have a heart attack Kaminsky would probably book me for bringing him the doughnuts.

I swung on over to get Doc and we headed across to Thelma's place. You could tell by the way she came to the door that the bell had woke her up and she began to squawk about my early arrival time until she noticed Doc standing behind me then politely invited us in. While I was filling her in on what we were doing there, she went for a robe. She had come to the door the way she went to bed, in a frilly, short, turquoise negligee. The memories set things in motion and I pretended to need the John until they calmed down.

Doc glanced around the room trying to look everywhere but at Thelma. He failed. Even first thing in the morning she managed to look damned enticing. She offered us coffee and toast and we both did a little preliminary looking around before we ate. After Doc said how good the coffee was for about the fourth time, we began our search in earnest. I found a shoe Thelma said she had long since given up for lost under the bureau. Doc came up from behind the radiator, red faced, holding up a lacy black brassiere. Thelma took it and smiled at him but offered no explanation of how it might have gotten there. I pictured her doing one of her stripteases for Steve, the way she used to do for me and caught her smiling at me, confirming my thoughts.

Doc raised his hand, like a school kid needing the bathroom, and when he was sure he had both our attentions let it drop, pointing to a spot where the linoleum didn't quite meet the woodwork by the hinged side of the bedroom door. A tiny spot not much bigger than a shell casing from a .32 automatic. Not much bigger at all, which is probably why no one had spotted it. Especially not the cops who performed a perfunctory search at best since they already had their suspect, nor the murderer who I would bet had hunted a whole lot harder than anyone else. But Doc Cutter was used to this kind of meticulous search, he never let illogical places blur his vision of logical possibilities. He was a master at examining the unobvious. As he stuck the tip of his pencil in the hollow end of the shell, picked it up, and slid it into an envelope, he had proved again just how good he was.

"I doubt it, but maybe we'll get a print on this," he said as he slipped the envelope into his inside sports jacket pocket.

"If we do, I'll bet it'll be Steve's. That gun was more than likely kept loaded, if I knew Steve Taylor."

"Guess you'll be right on that one, but I'll give it a shot. We could get lucky."

"That's not really the important thing though, is it, Doc?" I said in way of bringing my own hope up.

"Sure isn't," he offered happily.

"What are you two talking about, that's not the important thing," said Thelma all excited, "what could be more important than if there are prints on the shell or not?"

"Well, a .32 automatic doesn't throw its shells too far," Doc said in a very professional voice.

"So what?" Thelma was still in the dark.

"So, what Doc is trying to say is the shooter was standing near the door and it doesn't appear as if Steve tried to make any move off the bed. Which almost certainly confirms our suspicions that Steve knew his killer."

"That's great," she literally screamed, "let's take it to the cops. I can't wait to see the disappointed looks on the smug faces of those two Dicks."

Doc and I shot each other a glance. "Not so fast. We have to try to find out who it was first," I said, holding my right hand up like a traffic cop at a school crossing.

"Harry, you're always so damned cautious. Why wait, don't you think the fact that Steve probably knew his killer would interest Kaminsky and Riles?"

"Very much."

"So why don't we get this to them now?"

"Because even they are bound to remember that Steve knew you, too."

"So we're nowhere." All trace of confidence drained from her face and voice. Even her body, which had been quite animated while hopes of her proven innocence danced in her head, now sagged in sunken acceptance of a circumstantial conviction.

"Well, we can be reasonably sure it wasn't a random act of violence or a botched hold up," Doc said.

"That's a joke, Doc," Thelma said, almost laughing, "take a good look around this dump, we knew it wasn't a hold up coming in."

"That leaves us with someone Steve knew and it was probably not just some ex-client or mere acquaintance if he felt relaxed enough to be laying on the bed while talking to him. If my memory of Steve is correct, he treated his clients with a very professional attitude," I said shaking another Camel and theory to light.

"Yeah, Harry, when he had any," Thelma threw in with just enough disapproval of Steve to make me like it.

For the first time I realized how bitter and hurt she was by all this. Maybe things between Steve and her were not always a trampoline of roses. Funny, because even through our years together I had never before seen this vulnerable side of her so exposed.

"Hope I ain't interruptin' anything important," Sergeant Riles, Kaminsky's goon, said from the living room. "What are you doing at a police crime scene, Parker?" he spat. "And Doc Cutter," he glanced at his watch, "if I ain't mistakin' it's still business hours back at the good old 83rd."

"And if I ain't mistakin they still got a little procedure called knockin' before you enter a lady's apartment," I remarked.

"Gee, thanks for remindin' me, Parker, but the door was open so I. ... "

"Don't give us any of that jazz, Riles. No door was opened and there are three of us here to swear to it, see."

"Oh, yeah, and what a trio, too. Now let's see what we got ourselves here. We got us one murderer, one cop busted off the force for assaulting a superior officer and one bookworm cheating the citizens of their tax money runnin' around town while he's on the clock. You know, Harry, you got me shakin' in my boots. I guess I just oughta run out of here right now before I get myself into a real jam. Ha!"

Silence filled the room so loud my ear drums rang. It wasn't a superior officer, it was only Kaminsky I thought, but neglected to articulate.

"What's a matter, Parker, no smart quotes now?"

"Gee, Riles, I guess I'm all out. Now why don't you just tell us why you're here. Then you can leave, making the air fresh enough to breath again."

"Who says you get to stay?"

"I do," Thelma said, "he's workin' for me and he stays. Unless, you're thinkin' of arrestin' me again or somethin'."

"No. No bust. Not this time anyways." He looked at me, letting his facial expression show that he didn't care much for my being there, then he looked back at Thelma. "Suit yourself with him but it's a big mistake. And what about him," he said, pointing to Doc, "he workin' for ya too? It's against the law, ya know." He was now looking at Doc, "to work for private citizens and the City at the same time, Doc. You shoulda looked that one up in one of the penal code books at the precinct before you offered your services."

"And you should have checked my time card and noted it was punched out before you shot off your loud, stupid mouth, Riles."

It was the second toughest outburst I'd heard from the diminutive Doctor Cutter. I was proud of the guy and I hoped he wasn't bluffing because I was sure from the extreme redness now coloring Riles' face that he was going to check that time card as soon as he got back to the precinct.

Riles waited for his pressure to descend back through the clouds, tried, but failed to put a nothing bothered him smile on his ugly mug and turned back to Thelma.

"Just two questions we forgot to ask you, Mrs. Parker." He jabbed the Mrs. Parker down my throat with the skill of a sword swallower.

"Yeah, so go ahead." I was glad she didn't correct him.

"Did you know Mr. Taylor was having an affair with a younger woman?" He stressed the Mr. and the younger with a perfectly sharpened skewer. He had taken out his note book and stood prepared to jot down her response.

"Yes," Thelma said, looking at what seemed to be a very important piece of linoleum. I felt myself wince. I looked at Doc. He was fidgeting with a tube from the radio, his eyes searching for a spot in the apartment void of all human habitation.

"Did you know her name was Ruby, and that she owned a bar on Sterling Place?"

No emphasis was needed and none was given. The question in itself was enough. I looked at the tin flower-embossed ceiling and prayed.

"Yes."

My prayers died way short of God's ears with her answer.

"Thanks, ma'am. That'll be all. For now."

Riles smiled a real shit-eating grin, close enough to my face to let the bad eye know how happy he was. He closed the book, turned and walked out whistling a merry tune.

I stood and stared at Thelma for a minute, struck dumb by her heretofore unadmitted admissions.

She took a cigarette from her purse and struck three matches lightless before Doc came to her rescue with his lighter. She smiled at him. A smile that had its nervous beginnings with the anticipation of my verbal assault.

"How the hell could you leave me open for a blind side like that?" I didn't disappoint her smile that was forming suddenly into an angry barrage of its own.

"Look, I just didn't think it would come up. Okay?" She could still get louder than me when she wanted.

"Okay. Okay. Shit, no, it ain't okay! You didn't think it would come up! What the hell did you think Kaminsky was going to be doing with information like that once he found out?"

"Who knew he'd find out. You're always saying what a bum detective he is."

"Damn, Thelma! Any shithead worth his weight in dog do coulda found that crap out."

"You didn't!"

I started toward her, all the old nights of fighting and words passed between us percolating in my memory. Doc stepped right in front of me with some suggestion about calming down that I didn't quite hear. He did manage to stop my advance by standing there and lighting up one of his Old Golds. I wasn't about to push the little guy. Not even to get at Thelma. Thankfully, for all concerned, he knew it too.

Doc's hand caught my eye. He had lit two smokes and now offered me one. I took it and walked toward the window and gave the outside world some of my glare.

Thelma stamped to the kitchen. Like two fighters to the neutral corners we stood, each waiting for the other to fall or make a move. I watched some school kids, on their way to Saint Agnus, pulling off each other's caps and ear-muffs and playing saloogie. The little guys never stand a chance.

"Look, Harry," she said, blinking first, "I'm sorry about not tellin' ya the truth, it's just hard, you know, admittin' he was cheatin' on me, especially to you, after all we went through and all the things we ... I, said to you."

It was a big move on her part. It wasn't going to help her any with Kaminsky, but it was a big concession for her to make, especially to me.

"You hurt yourself's all." My voice was surprisingly calm and low. "I'm not poking around trying to find out about you and Steve. Believe me, I don't want to know," I said, "but by not telling me things like that it hurts the way I investigate and it might hurt with Kaminsky if he questions me and catches me off guard. That's all."

"Do you realize that these are the first calm words we've said to each other since. ... "

"Since the day I walked in and saw you hangin' off the bed and Steve at the same time."

Doc blushed and busied himself turning the pages of a three day old newspaper. Thelma and I seemed to be in the throes of a new dilemma. We were beginning to sense a calmness with each other that hadn't existed in years. After fully digesting all the three day old news he could Doc started for the door but I told him we'd better keep looking to see if we could come up with something else. Thelma asked if we were finished with the bedroom and when we both said we were, she went in and closed the door behind her.

"Weren't you a little rough on her, Harry?" Doc said low enough to make sure that Thelma couldn't hear him.

"Not half as rough as Kaminsky's gonna be, or some sharp prosecutor if it gets to that." I brushed some dust off the lamp shade and tightened the little gizmo that holds it in place.

We started hunting around for anything that even slightly resembled a thread of hope in clearing Thelma. We drew a blank.

She emerged fully dressed in a simple black dress just as Doc and I were finishing up with the couch and chair cushions respectively.

"I have to make arrangements ... for Steve's. ... "

It wasn't going to come out. Not yet anyway.

"We understand," Doc said, understanding for both of us. "We were just getting ready to leave ourselves."

"I'd like to borrow this a while," I said, holding up her address book.

"Why?" she asked without any objection in her voice.

"Just a long shot, see if maybe there's someone in it who don't belong. Ya mind?"

"Go ahead." Her right hand did that kind of automatic little twist out and to the right that seems to accompany some words of agreement.

We all kind of drifted out together. Doc offered Thelma a ride but she declined preferring the quiet solace of the subway. Maybe it was the company or maybe it was just the memories of the old Buick but, either way, I took it as an insult. I'd bet seven, well, maybe six million of the other eight million people in New York City would have preferred riding with Doc and me in the big old Buick over that dirty, crowded train any day of the week.

I got sucked in by the hum of the Buick's engine as we rode east up to the canal. A couple of sea gulls skimmed the surface, sniffed nothing edible through the garbage and the dead, and skirted toward the open water.

I had asked Doc to drive so I could thumb through Thelma's address book. He was singing along to some tune I thankfully didn't recognize. I had also let him tune my radio to his station and was now listening to an awful song about love and forever, and the same old crap cranked out year after year. A kid riding a bike shot out of nowhere and Doc's short stop, even at his safe speed, sent the book flying from my hands. I picked it up and put it back in my jacket pocket. The kid fell, from fright or a sharp stop of his own, but he hadn't been hit. Doc and I got out to see if he was all right.

"You big bozos oughta look where the hell you're goin'," he growled with all the sweetness of the canal behind him.

He was fine. We got back into the car. Doc had a kind of funny look on his face and I just knew what he was going to say.

"Harry, where the heck are we headed, anyway?"

He didn't disappointment me.

"I don't know either, Doc," I said near laughter..

We parked on Smith Street and got out and stood throwing rocks into the canal, hoping we didn't hit anybody we knew. A coal barge went by and Doc said, "Remember seeing one of those when you were a kid?" I knew what he meant and smiled staring at the slow movement of the fat, flat bottomed boat.

I thought young-kid thoughts of yelling and cursing at the old guys who rode the barges. How we would throw rocks at them, then run alongside the barge. The old guys, probably no older than I am now, would throw lumps of coal at us as we ran. The madder we got them the more they'd throw at us. We'd just run along cursing for all we were worth, dodging the coal and maybe even throwing up our fingers, on a particularly brave night.

Then, after the barge was completely out of distance, we'd go back and pick up all the coal the guys had thrown at us and bring it home to feed the old pot-belly stove. Your mother would smile at the good fortune you'd had at finding some coal along the banks of the canal. Your father would give you that extra special little wink if you had managed to get the coal without a mark on you. Proud you had been able not to get hit maybe even telling you of a time or two, when your mother had left the room, of how he had done the same thing as a kid along the old canal. Of course, his barges moved faster, and his old men threw harder and had better aim, but maybe if I'd have had a kid my exploits would have been exaggerated too.

"Harry?"

"Yeah, Doc."

"Thelma's up against it good." He obviously hadn't been thinking the same soft coal thoughts I had.

"I know," I agreed. "And Kaminsky ain't about to cut her any slack either." I stared into the dark brown stillness, an eerie winter sun reflected in its rippleless wake. Thinking that Thelma was in it as deep as the guys below trying to look up through the darkness to see what kids were running along the embankment dodging the hard thrown coals.

"You wanna go to the lab and see if there's anything on the shell?"

"Too early, Doc. You're out sick remember? Kaminsky would raise holy hell if you went back now and did non-department work. Especially, Harry Parker non-department work. By the way did you really punch out?"

"Sure, Harry. I wouldn't leave the building without doing that."

I smiled. The last honest guy in the Police Department and he wasn't even a cop.

"Let's go to my office and think this over till it's time to see Cudge."

"No candy conversations with Syd though, Harry, promise!"

"Okay, you big baby. Tough guy like you, backs down a hardened dick like Riles but can't take a little candy talk with a sweet little family man like Syd."

"Harry, some things are funny and some are not. Syd's fervent desire to be 'Number One Candy Man of Brooklyn' is totally lacking in the comedic aspect."

"I bet you enjoy cuttin' up frogs though, Doc."

He looked at me with a look that said, "Yeah but what does that have to do with anything." We both just decided to ride the rest of the way to Syd's in silence. Show tunes bouncing off the hard thinking edges of our minds.

Syd was talking with two old biddies from up the block as we entered the store. They stopped the gabfest as soon as Doc and I walked in. We heard them start up again, a little lower, as soon as we hit my office. Syd, ever the salesman, came back and asked if we wanted anything. After he had brought us our coffee and buttered rolls he rejoined his morning guests who were nursing their coffees better than a virgin with her first suitor-bought beer.

Doc looked at the window. "You know Harry," he said, "man your age needs a hobby, you know, something besides business."

"I know what a hobby is, and I got one. Drinking. It keeps me out of trouble."

"In it's, more likely."

"Doc, you worry too much. Besides, I thought we were supposed to be thinking about Thelma's troubles, which right now make mine seem like nothing in comparison."

I turned and leaned my chair back against the desk. It was a good feeling even if nothing was coming into view yet. I lit a smoke, shook the match and watched as the first puff exhaled up to the ceiling. Nothing blowing in that wind either. Maybe I was trying too hard. Maybe I just have to sit back, stare, and let it come to me.

Syd came in to tell me Cudge was on the phone. I thought Doc was going to have a heart attack when he heard his voice. He looked a little less pale as Syd walked out with me.

"Harry, is something wrong with Doc?" Syd asked. "He looks like he's got gas, maybe."

"He's fine. Syd, thanks for askin'."

"Don't know where this guy came from, or who he is," Cudge said as soon as I picked up the receiver, "but he got the straight dope, first time out of the box, Harry. Every word of it's gospel."

I expected him to say exactly that, but it somehow shook me just the same.

"Nothing on who he is, huh, Cudge?"

"Not much to go on, I mean I'll grant you there ain't too many six-foot-seven guys walkin' around town, but the ones that are, are all accounted for if you know what I mean."

I didn't really know what he meant but I said yeah and listened while he told me about two and a half million feet of electrical wire running through the great Empire State Building before we both hung up.

I paddled on back to Doc and told him what I'd learned, omitting the part about the wiring.

"About what you expected, ain't it?" He knew me better than I thought.

"Exactly what I expected, but for the life of me I don't know why."

"Because no sap was going to lay false information at your doorstep that could be so easily checked. Your only mistake was going to see Miss Collins before you had confirmed your facts with Cudge. But at least you got lucky there. If the big guys information had been wrong you'd have looked like a damn fool, Harry."

"Yeah. I was a bit too eager to tell her about Mason, wasn't I?"

"Yeah, just a bit. But all's well that ends well."

I thought about that as I sat back down, but had the bad realization that nothing had really ended. Especially not well. I suddenly felt that there were very real possibilities besides Mason after all. It was like a punch to the gut when I realized that it was beginning to look like a just-too-perfect-fit. And that I could now be left further out than I'd been since day one, with only a little more than one day to go.

I hated myself because I may have wasted so much time chasing down a false trail because I wanted so bad for it to be the golden path. Granted, he wasn't entirely out of the woods yet, but the way things fit too perfectly on Thelma made me start to think that there was just one too many coincidences pointing at Mason as well. It was like a series of coincidences, pins stuck in Mason's hide as if they were strategic places on a map, places dumb old Harry Parker was being led to one after the other.

A strip of light slanted through the brown patches on the window and reflected the telephone wire from the pole out back. The long thin shadow ran along the floor. I thought of Cudge saying something about President Hoover, way over in Washington, throwing a switch and lighting the Empire Tower the day it opened. I reached into my top desk drawer, searching for and finding two very thin pieces of metal.

"Come on, Doc," I said, "we've got to take a little ride." I was all excited.

"What's up?" he asked, startled by my abruptness.

"A hunch. A hunch about a too well confided story and a piece of wire hidden in plain sight." He shot me a puzzled look but got up just the same.

We grabbed our hats and got the wrong ones. If Syd had walked in then he would have sworn we were doing a bit from an old Laurel and Hardy movie. Doc's head was drowning in a sea of seven and a half and I must have looked like Mr. Potato Head in his small yellow cowboy hat.

When we got to the car I made sure that I was the one behind the wheel. I was too keyed up to crawl along at Doc turtle speed observing every traffic regulation on the face of the earth. Doc kept asking where we were headed and all I would say was, "You'll see." I somehow felt that if I told him what my hunch was it wouldn't pan out.

As we got within a few blocks he realized and said, "How are you planning on getting in?"

I took the two metal strips from my pocket and grinned as I showed him. He groaned something about breaking and entering, which I pretended not to hear. I pulled in about a block shy and we walked the rest of the way to Joe's Place, turning in every direction to make sure none of Kaminsky's boys were watching it. A precautionary waste of time given who we were dealing with.

The lock tumbled like a two dollar babe on a soft mattress. The air was dead and stagnant and held the stink of beer and smoke of a few thousand odd nights. I walked right back to the corner booth where I had sat with Ruby. Doc followed. I turned over the table. Nothing.

"At least be quiet about it will ya," Doc said, nervous and right.

I took my knife out of my pocket and cut through the plush material at the back of the booth. Nothing again. I cut up the seat even though I knew it couldn't be there. I was right.

"That's 'willful destruction of property'!" Doc informed me with a scornful look borrowed from any and every one of the Good Sister's of Saint Joseph.

"I somehow don't think Ruby's going to file a complaint, Doc," I answered much the way I had in school, proving why I now had nothing to show for my life.

I slumped in the one chair that faced the booth ready to admit I'd been wrong when I saw the tiny overhead light that stayed unlit. I stepped up on the chair and put my hand in.

"BINGO," I smiled down at Doc, who was checking the door for intruders who may have picked up on the loud vibrato sound of my voice ringing in success.

I showed him the microphone and traced its brown wire up through the chain that supported the light to the dark ceiling and over toward the bar. It came down intertwined in a hanging decoration and connected to a tape recorder behind the bar right where old friendly Phil was standing the night I'd been treated to an Academy Award performance. And probably where he always stood on evenings of "live" performances. Next to the recorder there was a beige box that looked like a listening device which I imagined allowed Phil to hear the conversations at the same time they were being recorded. I picked it up and found that it also had a switch which allowed him to turn it off so no one approaching him would hear the deep inhaled breaths of the very heavy breather, Ruby.

The cops who tossed the place had probably had little knowledge of devices electrical and just figured the thing was used when Phil and Ruby wanted some music but didn't want to feed the jukebox. There was no tape in the machine, and my bet was that that was what Ruby and Phil had delivered to 65th Street on their last night on earth.

I remembered Phil said T.M. always sat at that booth with his brickyard blonde and drank champagne. More than likely it was T.M. and Ruby and I'd bet the combination of champagne and low cut dresses Ruby wore could get a man talking about business. Maybe even to the point of insider trading shady business. I filled Doc in on all my suspicions.

"A good line for blackmailing Harry, but why the kidnapping?"

"Give me a minute to be proud about what I got before you tell me what I ain't got, will ya, Doc?"

I reached behind the bar and came out with a couple of bottles of beer. Doc looked at his watch and decided to ignore it. My watch told me to do whatever the hell I wanted. It had been a rather promiscuous piece from the moment I strapped it on. We sat at the bar for quite a while figuring out little except how many times eight or nine warm beers make you hit the can.

"I think, at least for now, this place has told us all it's going to, Doc." I offered up after what I hoped was my last trip to the john.

"Probably right. Where to now?" He was suddenly anxious to get going.

"To see J.E."

"What's she got?" he asked as we both rose and replaced our hats and coats, bracing for the cold journey ahead.

I decided against going for the obvious. "Well, maybe she can take a look at T.M.'s check book. Might as well follow up on the blackmail angle, it's all we got for now. See if Ruby was getting any checks on a regular basis."

I took a couple of six packs and two unopened bottles of bourbon from behind the bar and asked Doc to hold them as I relocked the joint on the way out. He shook his head but said nothing. I guess he figured I was right about Ruby not complaining. The Buick was beginning to know the way to Pierrepont Street. I only hoped it wasn't getting any spoiled notions. Next thing you'd know it would want premium gasoline and regular oil changes.

CHAPTER 18

"Miss Collins ain't home." Charles took great pleasure in telling us. "And I don't know where she went so you can fuckin' beat it," he had no trouble adding.

"Oh, Charlie boy, Miss Collins ain't gonna like it when she hears the way you treated us after we came all the way over here with good news about her old man."

I gave him my best poker bluff grin, turned and walked away with Doc on my heels. Charles, after a slight pause, calling us back for all he was worth. The Buick never seemed warmer than driving down that block watching him run, without a jacket, alongside the car, trying to get me to stop. A slight acceleration to sixteen miles an hour kept him chasing without catching up until he ran out of gas.

"Not in as good a shape as he looks," Doc matter of factly commented as he shook a smoke from its pack.

"Yeah, but I still don't think I'd wanna tangle with him," I said with more than a little truth in my voice.

"You seem to push for it just the same," he said while looking back at Charles through the rear window.

He was right. I'd have to admit to myself that Charles and I were never going to enjoy life's little pleasantries together. No sharing pool room, three corner bank shot congratulatory pats on the back or poker nights out with the boys, just wasn't meant to be. I stopped the car and watched in the rear view for Charles to come up almost even with the trunk, then gunned it. As long as we weren't going to be friends. ...

Farrell's was an early-opening joint, catering to the lunch time crowd as well as the late night drunks and we just kind of found ourselves there. The Buick was getting to know its way to a lot of places around town. Farrell's though was the first place it had learned to take me to and from without the need of my attention.

I was surprised to see Joe behind the bar at this time of day. I wasn't surprised by the fact that he was talking up a blonde who could have fit Phil and Ruby's mythical description of T.M.'s girl-friend to a T. He looked up when we came in and one finger motioned to the spot behind the bar where he kept the beer. I got the hint that the dame was another special one and reached over and pulled six then me and Doc hit a table. Jack Batson, a regular patron I had spoken with on many occasions, was at the bar and told me, without my asking, that Ed, the usual day man at the stick was out with "some bug." I thanked him for the low down and headed toward Doc.

"No glasses, Harry?" Doc mildly complained.

"The beer's in bottles, Doc. Bottles are made of glass. They do that so you don't need glasses. Besides, how many hands you think I got? It was either four beers and two glasses or six beers. Using my executive decision making powers, and seeing that Joe was far too busy to be washing any dishware I opted for the extra two beers. We can decide if it was the correct decision after the first four are gone."

After what seemed like no time at all I was over for another six. Joe didn't bother to look up. The blonde was laughing at one of his lines. She had one of those ersatz, "Oh you're so funny" laughs that most men will only hear in a background sort of way. The guy should take out a patent. When I got back to the table Doc had no further questions about the glasses so I figured I had made the right decision on that score at least.

"You know," Doc was saying before I was fully in my seat, "why should we care where this new big guy came from, I mean now that Cudge's confirmed what he gave us, what's the point in worrying?"

"Might be a set up. One or two pieces of the straight dope, then bingo, led down the wrong trail. And some wrong trails can be rather permanent."

We sat through another round lobbing out theories about the big guy, Ruby, and T.M. like they were softballs arched up for easy homers over at the Parade Grounds. Then Doc tapped my bottle with his and pointed toward the bar. Joe was pointing at us and J.E.'s eyes were following his lead.

She walked toward us with every eye in the joint following her progress. She was as totally unaware of herself as others were aware of her. She looked to, not at us as she came and didn't bother to ask if we would mind her joining us when she got there. She just sat at one of the unoccupied chairs assuming her voyeuristic right into our ordinary lives. She glanced at the empty bottles with dubious expense account tolerance.

"Syd knows you well," she began, explaining how she found me. I would have figured it out, but I didn't feel like cutting into her speech to let her know it.

"Charles was very upset when I got home. He said you treated him badly, Mr. Parker. Refused to divulge some very important information you had about my father."

She paused. She didn't exactly say it like a question so in place of an answer I nodded her on.

"Well, Mr. Parker, do you have some very important information about my father, or not!?"

She could deliver her questions and commands in the same manner. Impossible to tell them apart. I didn't like her demanding rich girl "do-it-for-me-now-boy" character trait one bit and took a long pause before answering to let her stew a minute.

"I'll know more about how important the information is after you let me sift through your father's personal papers," I said very calmly. Then took a long, head tilted back gulp from the cold, wet bottle of Rheingold clasped in my hand.

"And what makes you think I am about to allow you to do that!?" She stuck with her same attitude. The one that had probably carried her through most of her spoiled, snobby little rich girl life.

"You either want Daddy back, or you don't." I was as casual and easy about my response as she was uptight about her question.

The quantity of beers consumed prior to and after arriving here helped tremendously.

Doc was being very good at reading the Rheingold label and not helping me. He was holding his bottle in both hands, like holding both of his young lover's hands in his. He stared at the bottle as if into her eyes. Either he'd become very good at minding his own business, or....

"What is it you are looking for, Mr. Parker?" J.E. broke into my thoughts, her attitude turned down a notch or two, she now seemed almost human. It took me a second or two to realize she was speaking to me. As I was adjusting to her more gentle demeanor Joe came over with a glass filled with a pale green, dry concoction and gently placed it, on a coaster, in front of J.E. She looked up at him.

"Compliments of the house," he said in his smooth, soft voice that he reserved for working the women.

She smiled slightly and took a sip, then turned back to me without a word to him, which signaled his dismissal better than a pink slip in the depression. Joe wasn't Joe for nothing; he chatted up three different babes on his way back to the bar, never a wasted trip for Joe.

"First time I ever saw him out from behind that bar when there wasn't a fight going on," Doc offered.

J.E. paid no attention to the significance of Doc's statement and asked again what I thought I'd find among her father's effects. She said "effects" the way a lawyer does at the reading of a will and I wondered if she knew something more about her father than I hoped.

I slid my chair back and stood, waiting for her to pick up on my lead. She didn't budge. Follow the leader was obviously a game she'd never learn to play.

"I could search your entire house," I said, "but as we both know that could take till Christmas and T. M. sure ain't got that long. It would be a lot easier if you came with me and showed me where he keeps his papers."

Her chair scraped begrudgingly along the wood floor. Everyone in the joint turned in our direction. She got up and we started toward the door. I dropped some money on the bar and Joe gave a quick wave and yelled "Thanks, Harry" when he spotted the tip. I wasn't having fun with J.E. and decided she owed Joe a fiver for her attitude.

Charles was sitting in the limo, double-parked just outside the door. The snarl on his mug was a match for Dante's worst imaginings. I tipped my hat in his direction as Doc and I walked by on our way to the Buick.

Charles drove slowly, taking Fourth Avenue over to Fulton then turning onto Pierrepont. He was lighter on the pedal than Doc, though I guessed that was reserved for when J.E. was in the car. There was a spot half way up on the right hand side of the street too small for Captain Charles of the H.M.S. Janet Elizabeth but the Buick slid in with ease.

Charles stopped in front of the house and ran around the car to let J.E. out reminding me of a laboratory rat running through a maze. Doc and I caught up and went into the house with J.E. while Charles went back to find a spot big enough to dock the ocean liner.

J.E. put her gloves on the marble pedestal, her hat on an antique chair that looked like it would die of mortification and lack of support if you even considered sitting on it, and threw her jacket on another stronger chair. She was damned used to having people pick up after her and I got the feeling that's what I was doing with the T.M. case. Just picking up a mess; a mess, perhaps, created by J.E.? Funny how little things like dropped gloves, hats and jackets can get you thinking of bigger things like missing fathers, unappreciated boyfriends and million dollar payoffs.

We went into the library. It was a huge, two-story job, with miles of leather and wood. Doc walked along one of the long walls fingering bindings, stopping often, nodding his head, impressed with the gold embossed titles. I admired the blending of rich, dark cherry, teak and all the wonderful woods of the world. The beamed cathedral ceilings were divided from the walls by a stained glass perimeter of fourteenth-century heraldic motif. It struck me that T. M. Collins had probably never been a Boy Scout or dreamed he was Tom Sawyer fishing the mighty Mississip or even broken in a baseball glove for that matter. His dreams must have always been on a grander scale. I took up residence in a plush leather chair that wrapped itself around me with the comfort of a baby's blanket when I sat. Everywhere I looked the high polished richness of the room struck me silent with the awe of its grandeur. J.E. slipped through a door at the far end of the room, presumably to get to T.M.'s papers.

Charles walked in and gave us his best prison yard stare-down treatment. I couldn't help but wave casually and ask what time dinner was being served.

"I don't know, what time's the mission open?" He was so clever.

J.E. came back and Charles dissolved out the door. She had folders in her arms and laid them on a huge oak table designed for conferences in a large corporation, but it was probably used by T.M. to tidy up loose ends or thumb through the Wall Street Journal or the Sunday Times. She spread the papers from the first two folders on the table and I sat down and went to work. Boring stuff that for the most part I didn't understand. Although, "buy" and "sell" were two words I did recognize and they came up quite frequently. It was folder number three that gave me what I wanted, a separate check book with one thousand dollar monthly payments to Miss Sally Mancusso. I showed the canceled checks to J.E. and Doc and let the looks on their faces reflect my joy.

My smile disappeared entirely when Doc said, "Still don't show why the grab on T.M., Harry."

"I know that, Doc, but we're getting there. Maybe something went wrong with the monthly arrangements. Maybe whoever's running this show got greedy and wants one big million dollar pay-day all at once."

"You think there was someone else in on the blackmailing, Mr. Parker?" Miss Collins asked with arched eyebrows.

"Very definitely. Ruby here ran a dive in a bad neighborhood. She lived in a dump and didn't have much in the way of a bank account, in either name. Phil had even less. A thousand a month is an awful lot of dough to have nothing to show for. Which means there's got to be somebody takin' a very large slice off the top. The real person running the show. Besides someone has to be holding T.M. somewhere."

"How did you know about the bank accounts, Harry?" Doc was inquisitive.

"One of the benefits of having early rising neighbors is that you have a lot of morning hours to play with. I dug up some low contacts in high places I'd met during my days on the force and looked into the bank accounts of both Phil and Ruby as soon as we found out that they had aliases and my inquiries came back with the right answers. Sorry I didn't mention it, Doc, I've been thinkin' about the implications and kind of got caught up in my own deductive prowess."

"Are you any closer to realizing who the person who's 'running the show' is, Mr. Parker?"

"I have some more checking to do, Miss Collins, but an end is in sight."

"May I remind you that tomorrow midnight is also very much in sight," she replied sarcastically.

"You may, but you needn't. I am well aware of the day and the time for that matter." Since T.M. obviously didn't want to be bothered by time in his library and had no clock in the big room, I was only aware of the time if my watch had suddenly been struck with accuracy, which had about the same chance as me or Cudge riding winners in the Kentucky Derby.

"Come on, Doc, and bring your shovel. Miss Collins is understandably concerned with how fast we get to digging. Good day, Miss Collins."

She smiled a rather placating smile and shoved her father's papers back into their folders. Neatness and sense of order were not among her strong suits. Doc and I found our way from the library to the front door, no easy feat without our trusted Gargantuan guide.

"What made you think to check their bank accounts?" Doc asked while we were waiting for the Buick to warm up.

"Like I told J.E., Doc, someone has to be stashing T.M. somewhere. By checking their accounts and seeing how little they actually got to keep, it was easy to tell that that someone was not Ruby. Phil had nothing of what could be called assets either and he was also getting a pension from the Fire Department, which meant if he was getting any kind of real bucks at all out of this he'd have something stashed away. And he didn't so that let him out too. The person getting the big take is quite obviously the one running the show and from the accounts I've seen we don't have that person yet."

"Beautiful deduction, Mr. Holmes."

"Elementary, Doctor Watson."

We pulled out and headed to my place. Mrs. Geetus must have been out as we climbed the steps unencumbered by her reproach. We went in my room and I pulled all the cold cuts and condiments from the Coldspot and spread everything out on the table. I grabbed two plates from the cabinet, happy I had washed everything. Threw in two glasses for the beer, a small consolation to my lunch guest, and we built us some Dagwoods and listened to Mr. Bellem, home from work, speaking in hushed condescending tones, which meant he was probably speaking to some dame on the telephone in the hallway. At one point we heard the word "notes" very clearly. I smiled and Doc shook his head intuitively knowing my notes were the topic of discussion.

There was a rap at the door and the big man didn't wait for my "come in."

"I believe you still owe me something," he said. "Got any new assignments?" he wised through his Cheshire grin, as I paid up.

"Yeah," I said and smiled back not as pretty or as wide. "Find out who two cops named Rogers and DeLuca were workin' for and if there's a link between that guy and the couple that did a 10.0 three-twisting swan dive off an apartment house roof over on 65th Street."

"That's what I like about you, Parker, you ask such easy questions. Get back to you soon, this may cost double though." He let the last part out like a question frightened by the sound of its own voice, pausing petulantly to see if I'd go that much. Since it meant solving the case I'd have gone a whole lot more.

"A little steep," I said, "but it might be arranged."

He walked out with the big cat smile back on his ugly kisser.

"Harry, a yard for information Cudge will give you for a five spot?" Doc was amazed at my sudden generosity.

"Cudge doesn't deliver as fast as this guy, besides I said it might be arranged, not it would be."

"I don't think he's a guy you would want to cross," he said, the mother hen apparent in his voice.

"Be back in a minute," I said. "Wanna see if Cudge has anything on these two mugs yet."

I went to the phone in the hall. Bellem had given it up, at least for the time being. I dialed the hospital and asked for Mr. Congelluno. A nurse with a voice that sounded like she had a gag stuck in her mouth informed me that, "Mr. Congelluno has checked himself out. Against the doctor's wishes. No, he didn't say where he was going. But he was muttering something about a big man," she helpfully volunteered, firmament of flesh ringing in her every word.

"Cudge is onto something." I filled Doc in on his morning's activities as I walked back in on him as he was putting what we hadn't polished off back in the fridge.

"You think we should find him in a hurry, don't you?"

His voice was anxious and rushed. He closed the door to the fridge with a thud.

"I don't think he's going to do anything overly violent if that's what you're implying. I just think his pride's been hurt and he's tryin' to find out some info first's all."

"Yeah, but I think the info he's after is where to find the big guy. You know how Cudge can get. And she said he was after the big guy."

"Sure I know how he can get, he's never failed to collect on a loan, but she said he muttered something about a big guy, not that he's after a big guy. I just happen to think that it's the information gatherin' side of him that's hurt now and not the enforcin' side of him. Besides I asked him to wait on that remember, so even if the urge overwhelms him I don't think he'll get too violent."

"Hope you're right, is all," Doc said as he wiped the table clean. Watching him made me realize he saved all his sloppiness for the lab.

I hoped I was right about Cudge too, though I didn't bother adding it to the conversation.

"Where you off to?" Doc asked as I threw my hat on and headed for the door.

"Guess we'll pass by Farrell's again, Cudge does a lot of work outta there."

"Yeah, not a bad place to stop for a beer either."

"Doc, I believe you're corruptin' me."

I never bothered with all the warm up time Doc did and we were out of the parking spot we'd so recently sidled in to in a hurry. The streets passed quickly and quietly and before I knew it we were pulling up in front of Farrell's. We parked up the side street and walked around to the avenue and through the inviting doors. Thelma was at the bar and Joe was talkin' her up plenty. He waved his finger toward the beers and it took everything in me not to go over and break it off in mid-wiggle. Suddenly Joe's female forays didn't seem so trivial. I moseyed on over slowly, counting to myself, and wearing a smile as phony as any ever displayed at an Atlantic City beauty contest. I took Thelma by the arm and led her to a table while Doc reached for the brews. Joe was so shocked by Thelma's coming with me he failed to notice Doc reaching over the bar.

"Jealous that yet another man might steal my love, Harry?" She was deep into drunk. That funny kind of drunk where you believe that no one else can tell you're there.

"Nah, babe, the guy who steals your love commits only petty larceny." I wasn't drunk. "You didn't used to get drunk this early in the day," I couldn't resist adding.

"My lips ain't touched a glass all day!" She really believed she could pull it off.

"Been using a straw?" I couldn't pass up the opportunity, drunk or sober.

"Huh. So where you gettin' with my case? Any idea of who killed Steve, or have you stopped tryin', too busy with your rich dame from up The Heights?" She measured each word with the deliberate carefulness of those who have had too much to drink.

I suddenly remembered all the drinking nights of shrill voice fantastic craziness she could get in in the old days and why the love/hate feelings for her kept shifting gears in my mind and other places. I didn't feel much like reliving any of our mammoth matches so I just waited for Doc to come with the beers. She had something pink and lady-looking in her hand, contrasting perfectly with her attitude.

After Doc and I had each sucked down a couple of beers, Thelma made it apparent, by dangling her empty glass and giggling ungirlishly, that she was ready for another. I made it just as obvious by putting my bottle up to my mouth, tilting my head back, leaning back in my chair, and searching for cracks in the ceiling that I wasn't ready to play go fetch for her. Doc got up, took her glass and headed for the bar. I watched Joe reluctantly detach himself from a red haired conversation and throw the mixings in a glass that turned Pepto Bismol pink with his stirring. Doc padded back and gently deposited the concoction in front of Thelma.

"Thanks, Dociepoo," she slurred, "at least there's one gentlymen in the room." She gave me one of her very best, "so there" looks. I almost expected her to stick her tongue out at me.

I was about to say something about Steve but remembered that I was the one who wasn't drunk and decided to let it go.

"Well, what you got to say for yourself?" She wasn't being appreciative of my good natured ways.

"I say those little pink things must be a lot stronger than they look."

"Oh, you're a riot, Harry Parker. How about it, Doc? Ain't Harry Parker a riot? Maybe he should get himmmmm self a nightclub act, whattya think?"

"It seems as though he might be right, though, Thelma. About the drinks I mean." He defended my position as timidly as humanly possible.

"Right! Right! Well of course he's right, but what the hell's the point in that?"

Doc looked down between his hands. If I ever want to know what's written on a Rheingold label he'll be the man I'll ask.

Joe came over with another pink concoction and put it in front of Thelma.

"Fifth drink is always on the house," he explained showing more teeth than a shark, and failing to notice, that there was still plenty left in her fourth.

"Doc and I had nine beers each in here today, Joe, guess that means you owe us two each, huh?"

"It's a ladies only policy, Harry," he said, losing the smile and the low, polite voice that had been so apparent when he spoke to Thelma.

"Oh, Doc, I don't like the sound of that. Whaddya think all the guys are gonna think when we tell them about it?"

"I think they'll think, as we do, that it stinks. Probably start finding their way back to O'Keefe's again, Harry." Especially considering a lot more money is spent in here by men than women.

Joe brought four beers over. Enough, he thought correctly, to buy our silence.

Thelma lifted her chin off her ample bosom and put it in her hand, which was supported by her elbow propped up on the table. A rather elaborate set up for someone in her condition.

"You're not exclusive at all, Harry Parker." The words moved slowly through her clenched teeth.

I stared, waiting, watching her tongue roll around in her mouth in equal proportion to her eyes rolling in her head, knowing there was a punch line still forming in the deep recess of her drunken mind.

"No," she said, smiling, remembering, "you're everybody's fool."

I smiled too. The line would have been a lot more effective if she had managed to deliver it all at once but it was pretty good. And right now I was feeling like it wasn't too far off the mark either.

"Uh-oh," Thelma said shaking her finger back and forth as if she were admonishing a kid. Then, with eyes open extra wide she pointed over my shoulder. Riles was behind me, near the door, but he quickly closed the gap between us.

"Evening, Shamus."

"It's only afternoon, Riles."

"It's always later than you think, Parker. Get up. Kaminsky wants to see you. Now!"

"Kaminsky? Kaminsky? No, can't say as I've ever heard the name. I guess I'll have to decline, Bill. Unless, of course, I'm under arrest or something. Am I under arrest, Sergeant Riles?"

He put his hand around my neck from behind and squeezed the artery on each side, very tightly.

"No, Mr. Parker, you're not under arrest, but we know, being the righteous citizen you are, that you're just dyin' to help the police in any way you can. So, of course, we knew you wouldn't mind showing a little cooperation by coming down to the precinct to answer a few questions for Lieutenant Kaminsky, now would you?"

"Oh, you mean Lieutenant Kaminsky, now why didn't you say that in the first place, of course I remember Lieutenant Kaminsky." I turned to Doc and Thelma, "You both remember Lieutenant Kaminsky, don't you? The tall, light, skinny, ugly fellow who never met a lie he couldn't pin on somebody, or a truth he couldn't ignore?"

Riles grip tightened slightly. There hadn't been much room for improvement. I got up and Thelma said, "Harry, you don't have to go with this little ape if you don't want to you know, he ain't arrested you." She seemed to have sobered a lot since Riles entered the joint, but not quite enough.

"But he asks so politely, Thelma," I said with my neck still engulfed in hand.

"Ahw. He don't look so big to me."

"That's only 'cause you never looked at him with your eye full of fist."

Doc got up and dropped some money on the table and slipped his hat and jacket on.

"And just where do you think you're goin', runt!" Riles, like Miss Collins, had a way of forgetting to put question marks on the end of his questions.

"First, Sergeant Riles, my rank as forensics technician is higher than that of a mere sergeant. Second, I happen to be off duty anyway. Now, knowing both of these facts, don't you feel pretty stupid standing there asking me questions which you know you're not going to get answers to?"

God, you have to love this guy. I think I want to be like him when I grow up.

I left with Riles. Doc took my keys and followed in the Buick. Thelma was ordering another glass of pink happiness as we left and Joe was smiling like a kid in a candy store. Syd would have loved that smile. I didn't appreciate it much.

We drove quietly to the 83rd. Riles behind the wheel, steely eyes riveted somewhere between the road ahead and me in the rearview. I was in the back seat, behind the wire-mesh screened cage, hands cuffed, even though I wasn't "in custody" but still happy that Riles had come alone because it was sure as shooting that if someone else was driving he would have been in the back seat with me, massaging my ribs to the tune of something up tempo and loud on the car radio and the way my luck's been running some platter spinner would have picked that time to play a Krupa drum solo.

He pulled into a spot halfway up the block and dragged me at a quickened pace all the way to the precinct, past Pappy, who knew better than to look up from his True Detective, past the finger printing area, and the holding cells, up through the tuna/urine smelling stairs and right on down the hall.

"He didn't wanna come see ya, Lieutenant." Riles couldn't wait to get out of his rat bastard mouth as he pushed me through the door into Bernie's office.

"Now, Bernie, you of all people should know what a liar Riles here is. Me, not want to see my old pal, who could imag. ... "

I was beginning to recognize a small piece of the floor where one of the tiles was chipped in the corner. My face seemed to be meeting up with it quite frequently lately. Either Riles had uncanny skill in his ability to knock people into the same landing pattern, or he was the luckiest S.O.B. in the world. I felt my ribs. They were still there, set back an inch or so since the case had begun, but they were still there, for now anyway.

"Harry, did anybody ever tell ya that you ain't much good at makin' people real happy to see ya?" He wore an exasperated look.

"No, Bernie, you're the first, I swear to God."

Riles sapped me, harder than on the previous occasion, or maybe my head was just getting softer. All I knew was the ringing in my head was as loud as coal rushing down a chute.

"I bet he ain't gonna be the last to tell ya," Riles threw in, in way of an explanation for the sap, I suppose.

Doc appeared at the door.

"Not this time, Doc, get the hell out of here." Bernie was forceful.

Doc held up an envelope. "Sure thing, Bernie, I was just on my way up to see Captain Quiggly with Harry's photos here."

Kaminsky paused, thinking. He could only be weighing the, "Does Doc actually have these photos of Harry or does he have much bigger balls than I'd given him credit for," possibility. You could almost see the words run across his forehead like on that big electric light bulb sign down in Times Square.

"Stop askin' questions about a bunch of stiffs that don't concern ya!" Bernie shouted looking down into my face, a position he was certainly used to and one he definitely preferred. Then he picked up a folder from his desk and started reading, letting me know that our interview had concluded and that I was free to crawl on out, letting him get on with some truly important, official NYPD business. Like a graft collection list or the home phone number of a working girl in need of a favor.

"Well!" he said when I didn't get off the floor as fast as Jessie Owens in the four-forty, "what the hell you waitin' for, an effing engraved invitation?"

I guess Doc could tell that my head was really spinning because he helped me out of the office and down the stairs. I waited till we were out of the building and half way to the Buick before I asked him what he had in the envelope.

"Pictures, Harry. Would I lie to Kaminsky?"

"Don't ever remember you takin' any pictures of me, Doc," I said, still trying to button the last button on my coat.

"I didn't say they were pictures of you. I said they were your pictures." He gloated.

"You'll forgive me if I'm still thinkin' gray tiles and cracked ceilings, Doc, but it sounds like there's no difference there to me."

"Big difference. These," he said as he shook the envelope a bit, "are pictures taken outside the apartment house on Sixty-Fifth Street the evening of a certain 'lovers leap.' And I got these particular copies for you, so they are, in fact, your pictures, even though they are not pictures of you."

"Sounds a lot like my logic when it comes to clients' expenses is rubbing off on you, Doc."

"You pick up a little something here a little something there, that's the way life is." He was beaming pride from a lighthouse bright smile.

We got in the car and I decided to let it warm up a little longer than usual in hopes that what was left of my brain would unscramble. I was still staring straight ahead when Doc shook my arm and handed me the envelope. There were four pictures. Two shots showed the full length of the car, from each side, and the other two were close ups of the middle segment, the part where the bodies had landed, also from each side. The car looked like a car two people who had taken a dive off a six story building had landed on. The people on top of the car looked flatter than regular people. Although, since photography is a two dimensional art, that part could be contributed to my imagination. The street was busy with badly dressed men, proving they were all cops.

"What's that little object down there on the sidewalk, near the back wheel, Doc?" I pointed to a small blur.

"Someone had false teeth and coughed them up," he said and smiled knowingly.

"I'll bet it was Phil. There was nothing false about Ruby but her intentions."

I threw the car in gear and eased it out slowly moving her back and forth out of a space that had shrunk with the arrival of a too-friendly Chevy on my front bumper. It probably took me an extra few passes the way my head was pounding, but that was all right I was in no hurry. Doc was lost in thought, staring out the side window. He snapped out of it and asked where we were headed.

I said that since Cudge doesn't live too far from here we might as well go over and see if he's at home.

"What about Thelma?" he asked with no small amount of Joe's with her concern in his voice.

"She's a big girl now, Doc. Besides, I'll bet Joe will make sure she gets home all right, though I'm not sure whose home she'll get to."

Cudge wasn't home and it looked like he hadn't been. His blood stains hadn't been cleaned up in the hallway nor in his apartment and the place looked just like it did when Doc and I left it the other day. I'd once again picked our way in.

"He doesn't have the best of neighbors, Harry. Nobody thought to come in and clean up for him." He was actually surprised.

"Yeah, well, at least it don't look like anybody thought to come in and rob him either." I picked the door locked again. I was getting as good at closing it as opening it.

We were on our way down when we heard heavy footsteps coming up. I grabbed Doc's arm and motioned him back up. We went up past Cudge's floor toward the roof and my .45 was automatically in my hand as we crept back down. The big man stopped in front of Cudge's door and started knocking.

"I'll bet that ain't opportunity," I said, as Doc and I came down the few steps and headed toward him.

"Very funny, Mr. Parker," the big guy said, losing some of his self assurance as he glanced at the gun in my hand.

"You know I'd be terribly disappointed were I to learn that you were getting information from Mr. Congelluno here at his very reasonable rates and then passing it onto me at your very inflated prices. Very disappointed, indeed." I waved the gun a little, for effect. I knew it wasn't true because Cudge had said he didn't know the guy, but I figured it would speed his explanation of what he was doing here.

"I got a message that Mr. Congelluno was looking for me."

"What kind of message?"

"One I had to break with my Tom Mix secret decoder ring." He smiled, proud of his witty repartee.

I waved the gun a little harder.

"Telephone call. Guy said Cudgel'd be here," he said and looked at his watch, "right about now. Guy said that he wanted to see me so I came here to find out what it's all about. You know Cudgel, says he wants to see you, you come, right?"

I patted him down, quickly. He was clean.

"You're a brave man coming to see Cudge ... empty handed. Most people he's looking for make sure to bring a little gift. Not that it does them any good. But they bring it just the same."

"I didn't know if he preferred dry or sparkling. And as you say, the gifts don't seem to help anyway. Besides, I told you, we're old pals."

"Then you should know that Cudge likes Rheingold, extra dry," Doc said helping me again.

"Your boys Rogers and DeLuca were working for someone out of the 83rd."

"No shit, Sherlock."

"Not Captain Quiggly."

"Another piece of information obtainable without the use of a crystal ball."

"I'm all out of silver platters, Parker, why don't you use that ten pounds of fat between your shoulders for something besides a hat rack?"

You could tell I had put the gat back in my pocket. The bravado was still echoing off the hallway walls as the big guy shoved on past us and down the stairs.

"Why do you think he didn't just come out and give with the info, Harry?"

"I don't know, he's passin' up a hundred by not givin' over. There's somethin' we're missin', and in more ways than one."

We headed back down the stairs ourselves, stopping on the stoop long enough to have a smoke and watch the world walk by listening to Debussy, I think, straining through a nearby slightly open window. When we finished our smokes and Cudge was still nowhere in sight, we headed back to the car.

"Syd's or my place, Doc?"

"Mrs. Geetus has it all over Syd, Harry."

I felt like telling him he should get a look at Sarah bending for the Tootsie Rolls, but decided it was a thought I'd better keep to myself.

We made it to my joint in no time flat, and were greeted at the door by Mrs. Geetus on her way to old man Whelan's for dinner provisions. She saw Doc and smiled. I guess he just has that air of respectability about him so lacking in her boarders. Doc tipped his hat and her smile grew to meet the size of his brim. Lucky for her he's a small guy with a head to match or she would have cut her own ears off.

We went on up the stairs and dropped our coats and hats on the chair by the door as we went in my room. I took the pictures out of the envelope, threw them on the table and lit a smoke. Doc lit one too and went back over to the chair and withdrew a small magnifying glass from his coat pocket and brought it back to the table.

We went round and round, over and over, passing the pictures and the glass back and forth like two miners searching the darkness for the vein of existence. If there was something to be found in the pictures it sure as hell wasn't being found by us.

We half-heartedly looked a while longer but still saw nothing in the line of a clue. Doc was getting frustrated and decided it was time to head home. After gathering up our coats and getting out to the car I dropped him off at his place and cruised on over to Farrell's alone. I always think better with something in my hand and alcohol is the best thought inducer I've found so far.

After four or maybe five Southern Comforts, the case, cases, weren't looking any clearer and I figured I better call it a night myself.

The door seemed a little further away from the table than when I had come in. I tipped my hat to a woman who's head was an inch or so from meeting her table and found my way to the street. I let the Buick warm longer than usual thinking about Steve and how impossible it would have been for a stranger to get that close to him without his instinctive nature getting him off that bed. I put the car in drive and knew enough to let it have its way with regard to navigation.

Smith Street isn't especially wide, but in places where there are no parked cars on one or the other side of the street, two cars can drive down at the same time. The guy next to me was pressing the point by staying with me on my right for a longer stretch than anyone should think themselves lucky enough to endure. I was losing all of J.E.'s money I'd invested in a good drunk by sobering at an alarming rate. No matter how I varied my speed he stayed put. He waited till the last possible second as a parked car was coming up on his side to gun it and run me into a parked car on my left. A Ford coupe of a vintage fine wines would be in awe of.

In true Harry Parker luck the rain picked just then to come down in sheets, but at least the old Buick, which had stalled on impact, started right back up again and I was able to leave the scene of my very non-accident without the bother of any paper work. Insurance companies and police reports be damned. The Buick didn't look like it suffered too much damage and it was way past time for the antique Ford to be off the roads anyway.

If that car that rammed me, as nondescript as any I'd ever seen, wasn't an unmarked prowl car I'll eat my hat without benefit of condiments.

CHAPTER 19
SATURDAY, JANUARY 11TH

The wake-up shot stung my lips and tongue. I must have cut my mouth on something last night. Oh, yeah, that little ram job on Smith Street. Funny how the bad aspects of nights before always seem to come back to you even when you aren't trying very hard.

There was very loud, forceful knocking at the door. Charles or the big guy? I reached for my .45 and politely invited trouble on in. I lowered the gun when I saw Cudge in the doorway. His knuckles seemed red and raw. He hadn't knocked that hard. A smile grew on his face as he said, "I found your big man."

"Was he worth finding?" My smile grew to meet his.

"We had a very nice chat." He out smiled me.

He looked from me to the pictures on the table and walked over and turned them until they were facing him. The look on his face told me he saw right away what Doc and I had wasted a good portion of our youths trying to comprehend.

"Let's get some coffee going, Harry. You look like shit and we got a lot to talk about. We don't got it all yet, but I figure with what you know and the little I throw at you you'll be able to piece this whole damn thing together in no time flat."

I slipped into my god-damned-you-know-who-given slippers and went over to the sink and filled the pot. His faith in my abilities was inspiring. Unrealistic, but inspiring.

"Better fill the whole pot, Harry. And maybe give Cutter a call. And here, call him too."

He shoved a piece of paper at me with a name and phone number on it. I looked at him and he just nodded. I went out into the hall and made my calls. I hadn't recognized the name but I had a pretty good idea of who it might be and after speaking to him for just a minute I knew it was the big guy. I made sure to leave the change for the calls on Mrs. Geetus' table before going back to my room and getting a cup of coffee. The change on the table was beginning to add up as I had made several calls over the last two days. Pappy, over at the 83rd didn't really mind talking, as long as it was on the phone, the one he controlled at the switchboard. Neither did several ex-con friends I had gone light on over the years, a lawyer friend was also in a gabby mood and even John Mason had a few choice words when he saw I was getting someplace.

The pot was half gone and some of the excrement had already started hitting the fan by the time Doc arrived. He was followed shortly by Cudge's extra special, unannounced guest, who was followed by the big guy. The big guy's mouth looked a little puffy and his eyes were both a dark shade of purple, but it really didn't look like he took too much persuading to give over with what he knew. Doc seemed relieved to see him in such fine shape.

Cudge, it seemed, had been gathering information from all sources and did have a couple of facts I didn't. Obtaining facts was Cudge's strong suit, putting the facts together and developing conclusions based on them was mine. Don't ask me why, I could just plain reason things out. Even some of my ex-colleagues would have to reluctantly admit this was my forte. And more importantly, to me, even Captain James Quiggly had once told me I'd be a fine detective some day. Of course, he had meant a Police Detective as I was still on the force then, but it meant he believed in my abilities just the same. I was glad I had restocked the coffee at Whelan's because it wasn't long before I was brewing another pot.

Everybody was throwing information into the kitty, most of it I already had, but sometimes playing with the info is very helpful and pretty soon I realized things were beginning to add up. I was feeling pretty damned good about myself when nobody else knew about the recording stuff over at Joe's Place, the checks from T.M. to Ruby and a few other items I had. I felt it not only gave me my ante into the game but a big raise as well. I was feeling even better when nobody else was making the pieces fit like I was. Unfortunately, there still was no hard evidence so we sat through another pot brewing up a plan. Some more phone calls were made and after stalling around for what I felt was "just enough" time I was on my way over to the Collins place.

Charles answered the door and told me Miss Collins was expecting me and that she was in the drawing room. As he led the way I couldn't help but think why servants said things like, "Miss SoAndSo is expecting you," since you made the appointment you knew damn well Miss SoAndSo was expecting you.

"Stick around, Charlie boy, it's going to get busy around here." I couldn't resist. I could feel this was going to be my day. My very best day in a damn long time.

"Good morning, Mr. Parker. I hope, and assume, that your being here at this ungodly hour means you have some news, some good news, about my father."

"You hope and assume correctly, J. E." My Cheshire grin rose to meet my enthusiasm and I knew it was wider than any one that old fuzzball sitting in her lap would ever muster and he was from the same family of grinners.

"Well, what is it?"

"I'm afraid I'll have to ask you to keep your 'Lily of Whatever' shirt on just a little while longer, J.E. The others haven't arrived yet."

"Others? What others?" She was confused. I liked it that way.

"I've taken the liberty of inviting a few guests for our little brunch gathering. How nice, French toast. Better order up some more though. The other guests may be hungry too."

I sat at the big coffee table and poured maple syrup over a stack of French toast that looked as if it had just arrived from Paris. I dug in, forgetting my social amenities. J.E. rang her little bell and looked at me as Charles entered. She asked timidly, "Just how much toast will be required, Mr. Parker?"

"Oh, I'd say eight or nine more servings, at least. You are having some aren't you, J.E.? Yes, of course, you are, make it eight or nine, at least." I was playing the I've got the whole world in the palm of my hand feeling I had for all it was worth and it was worth a hell of a lot more than the money I was going to get for the job.

She looked at Charles and said, "Go ahead, Charles, have Cook prepare the additional servings."

The bell rang and I heard Charles change directions in the hall and head for the front door. Charles was already looking a bit piqued and he was going to have a busy day ahead of him.

Charles led two men into the library.

"Ah, Kaminsky and Riles, right on time. Come on in, boys." I gave Riles a big welcoming slap on the back, hard enough to pay back a smidgen of his questionings.

The boys had that traditional trench coat, worn hat, even more worn shoes look that made them so easily recognizable as bulls. They looked even more out of place than usual in their present luxurious surroundings. Riles pushed his hat back and even in this cold weather his forehead was perspiring.

"Parker, what the hell. ... "

The bell rang again, cutting Bernie's higher pitched than normal question in half and sending Charles galloping off on his horse again.

"John, how good it is to see you again, old sport," I said as Mason entered the room. He was his usual immaculate self and without intention knocked Kaminsky and Riles down another rung or two on the "how not to dress" ladder of acceptability.

I was feeling absolutely giddy with power. So glad to be the one playing the part of William Powell, rounding up all the suspects in one room, with the cops there to bail me out if anything went wrong, just like the ending to one of the Thin Man movies.

"Lieutenant Kaminsky, Sergeant Riles, this is Mr. John Mason, the notable attorney. And the charming lady seated on your left is Miss Janet Elizabeth Collins. Mr. Mason, the boys. Miss Collins, the boys. Oh, how rude of me, I forgot. You already know one of the boys, don't you, J.E.?"

"Why yes, Mr. Parker, I do, but how do you. ... ?"

"Which one of the boys are you familiar with, Miss Collins?" I had figured out which one but wanted her to come out with it for that extra little hammer over the head. I was really enjoying myself more than any person should have a right to.

"Why, Lieutenant Kaminsky."

"And how is it that you know the good Lieutenant, Miss Collins? You don't mind my kind of taking your part here for a moment, do you Mr. Mason?"

"Not at all, Mr. Parker." His voice was cordial and thick like he was speaking to an old school chum who wore the same tie, knew the secret handshake and had been in on the late night panty raid that no one ever got caught on and I had to admit I liked it.

"Please, go on, Miss Collins." I was getting so into my William Powell, Thin Man character that I was afraid I was going to start calling J.E. "Mommy" and scan the room for Asta.

"Well, Lieutenant Kaminsky had introduced himself to Father a couple of weeks or so ago." J.E. said. "Sold him some tickets, to the Policeman's Ball, I believe."

"Yes, and after that?"

"Well, when Father was kidnapped I remembered his name and called him. I told him I had a matter in which I did not wish to involve the police, a rather confidential matter, and asked if he knew of anyone who could not only handle a tough assignment but could be trusted to keep a confidence as well."

"Allow me to take a wild stab in the dark here, J.E. Good old Bernie suggested that I was the perfect man for the job?"

"That's correct. Although, he didn't exactly say you were perfect. It was more like you could somehow manage to stumble your way through the case."

I looked at Bernie, he was sneering broadly and nodding his head. I wasn't about to let this slight set back ruin my big moment.

"That's how I got your name," J.E. went on, "only Lieutenant Kaminsky said that it was very unprofessional of him to recommend anybody and asked that I not reveal to anyone where I had, I believe the phrase he used was, 'come up with you.'"

"Oh yes, that sounds like Bernie's phrasing all right. And it was very unprofessional of you, Bernie, also illegal, but you weren't going to let a little thing like that bother you, were you? Of course, it was very smart of you to come about the Ball, like there really is one, such a short time before the kidnapping and I'll bet you made damn sure that your name was heard by Miss Collins so she'd know who to call when the time came. Maybe even left your name and number with T.M., in case he ever needed anything. Uh Oh, that establishes premeditation doesn't it, Bernie?"

"You're actin' as if I knew the kidnappin' was coming, Harry." There was the slightest quiver in his voice.

"Oh, but you did, Bernie. You are, after all, you'll forgive my using this particular expression when referring to you, the one who masterminded this entire debacle."

"Ha, speculation's all it is. I'm afraid I owe you an apology, Miss Collins, it would seem that I made a great mistake in recommending Mr. Parker after all, this case was obviously way over his head."

"It would seem you did make a mistake, Bernie. You underestimated me. You never thought I'd catch on and be able to sort this whole thing out, did you?"

"Catch on to what? You're dreamin', Parker." The small earthquakes tremoring in his voice belied his words.

"No, Bernie. As much as I'd like to be, believe me, even with scum like you, I'd rather hang anyone than a bad cop, Bernie."

"You ain't hangin' anybody with your bad guesses and poor theories, Parker."

"Oh, but I am, Bernie, and not just for kidnapping either. There's a little matter of four murders yet to be discussed."

"Four murders. This is gonna be rich. How do I tie to four murders?" His hat was twirling in his hands and his face said he didn't really think this was going to be rich at all.

"Ruby and Phil, you remember them, Bernie, from Joe's joint over on Sterling Place. Well, it seems that Ruby was doing some nasty tape business with Mr. T.M. Collins. He has, let us suffice it to say, rather strange sexual appetites and Ruby being ... Ruby was able to get him not only to act them out but to discuss them later at a little table she had at the back of her joint. These discussions were tape recorded at the bar by her partner Phil and then those tapes were used as blackmail against old T.M. Not very original I'm afraid, but it worked just the same.

"You see, T.M. figured he'd be ruined if his escapades were known on Wall Street. Not that there aren't others there doing the same or similar things. They just weren't getting caught at it."

"So if he's being blackmailed, why the grab? And why figure me, and not Ruby?" Bernie asked with a sideways sarcastic grin that tried to lie about his guilt but only served to make it that much easier for me to go on.

"Good questions, Bernie. Ones I have to admit I was askin' myself for a while. But it all made sense as soon as I realized that you were in on it from the beginning. Then after checking certain bank accounts it wasn't difficult to see who was getting the biggest share of the pie.

"Ruby was tied to you as a snitch and she made one helluva huge mistake letting you know what was happening with T.M. My guess would be Riles here got that out of her somehow, but that's neither here nor there. Her real trouble started when she came to you for a bigger piece of the action and that's when you arranged to snatch T.M. for one big pay off. You wanted to make sure she wasn't getting frightened to the point of telling him you were in on it and it was also your golden opportunity to rid yourself of Ruby and Phil for good. After all, no use in takin' chances with two 'outsiders,' and bar flies at that. Rogers and DeLuca were a bonus being in the car below like that because you knew you'd have to get rid of them anyway. Rogers knew who Ruby and Phil were going to meet. You told him to pick them up and take them to the apartment you were keeping on 65th Street, and although DeLuca couldn't figure his way out of a paper bag, you couldn't be sure whether or not it was the kind of information that Rogers would share with his partner. He would know what was going on the minute those bodies hit the pavement. So you shoved a little harder and caught a lot of luck and they hit the car instead of the sidewalk."

"Again, Parker, just guesswork and conjecture. Where's your proof of any of this? Where's your smokin' gun, as the Chief used to ask us?"

"Well, Mr. Mason, here used to work with the D.A.," I was winging it, "and he got the bank accounts for us. Didn't you, John?"

Mason, who I had filled in with my phone call played his part well. He took an over-long drag on his cigar, blew smoke in Bernie's direction and stared silently at him as I went on. It was the best way he could play it. He was a lawyer, and at least by theory, wasn't allowed to lie.

"Mr. Mason was also able to find out that you had the lab investigation moved across town." Another exaggeration - I hadn't found out for sure who moved the case, "knowing that Doc Cutter and me's good friends, and that he'd sure as hell give me any info he got on the case."

"So, what the hell do a couple of effing deposits mean? Nothing. And cases are moved all the time."

"In and of themselves you might be right about the deposits, although, the amounts are a bit large, even for a police lieutenant on the take. And although infrequent, there have been some case switches. But there's more. ... Okay, you can come in now."

The big guy came through the French doors from the court-yard garden. Everybody gave him that kind of trying to stifle shock look you'd imagine an extremely ugly six-foot-seven guy would get.

"This is Mr. Divine. Oh, I'm sorry, you don't know Mr. Divine, do ya, Bernie? Mr. Divine, this is Bernie Kaminsky. He's a detective at the 83rd precinct; the one you've been hearing so much about. Bernie this is John Divine. He's a reporter with the Brooklyn Eagle. Mr. Divine is doing a piece on police corruption, and Bernie, you'll never guess who his very special source is. Go on, take a shot. It's a man you know very well, a man Captain Quiggly and Mr. Divine have been keeping a close watch on. Oh, come on out from behind those drapes, Captain, you must be stifling back there. There we are, that's better." The Captain had been the special unannounced guest in our little coffee pot go round. "Now where were we. ... Oh yes, I remember, the special witness. Well, as I was saying Bernie, he's a man Captain Quiggly and Mr. Divine have been keeping under wraps, as they say, for a couppla days now. Have you guessed yet, Bernie? No? I'll help you out a little, it's an ex-friend of yours. Well, that's not really much help either is it, there are so many of those running around. Okay, it's an ex-friend of yours that you thought was dead."

Bernie made no sound, no move except his eyeballs shifting from side to side.

"Still no help! I am surprised. Okay, here's the big one. It's an ex-friend of yours that you thought you had killed. Come on, Bernie, that's got to narrow it down a little."

Bernie moved now, but Quiggly stepped in front of him and took his gun before he could draw it. Riles moved too, but Cudge came from nowhere and dropped him like a swatted fly with one punch to the top of the head. It was a thing of beauty.

"Oh, I think you've guessed it now, Bernie, but for those in the room who may not have," I said as I scanned the room and drank in the eyes riveted on me, hanging on my every next word, like the true ambrosia of the gods. "It's Tom Rogers. That's right, Bernie, he didn't die when you threw Ruby and Phil at him. That's what you and I should have realized when we were looking at those pictures, Doc, Cudge saw it right away, there was hardly any damage on his side of the car. He did get your message though, Bernie. Your message that he was supposed to die and the funny thing about it is, he took it very personally. That's why ever since he came out of his coma early this morning he's been talking a blue streak to Captain Quiggly and Mr. Divine here." I looked at Doc. "That's why Mr. Divine didn't deliver the info in Cudge's hall, Doc. Rogers hadn't come out of his coma yet so Divine didn't know who Rogers and DeLuca were working for." I turned back to the rest of the room.

"Mr. Divine's entire account of the Collins case," I looked at J.E., "except for the insider trading and the sex angle, which there is no reason to divulge, will appear in today's Eagle."

"The fact that Mr. Divine is a reporter is how he was able to help me with some of the finer points of the case. He has the inside dope on a lot of things going on in Brooklyn and has been investigating police corruption for months. So you see, Bernie, it's a lot more than mere speculation."

"I am glad you solved the case, Mr. Parker, but your math is faulty," Mr. Mason said.

"And just what doesn't add up, John, old friend?"

"If Rogers is still alive, who's the fourth murder victim?"

I looked at Bernie.

"In a way, Mr. Mason, that's the saddest of them all. You see Bernie here was having me tailed by two cops named Levine and Delvecchio who changed shifts a lot but that doesn't really matter because through some research of my own I'm sure they had no idea why they were tailin' me, they were just doin' what their dear old lieutenant ordered them to. Anyway he found out that I was askin' the kind of questions that he thought were gettin' me too close to him regarding T.M. So he needed to throw me off the trail until he could collect the money and skip town."

"By the way, Riles, you were never going to get any of the money either. My guess is you were going to wind up like the others."

He gave me an exaggerated look of disbelief.

"Hey, don't believe me, but in case you're interested the name on the bell and on the lease on the apartment Bernie rented over on 65th Street is William Riles. No roads were supposed to lead back to Bernie. Incidentally, Bernie, the little hidey-hole in the back of your bedroom closet wasn't that great a spot. The tapes have been destroyed. But as I was saying, Bernie felt he had to have me sidetracked. And he didn't want me killed because then J.E. might panic and call in the FBI. So first, he tried to hang a frame on me by sending a guy who dropped a hot rod in my room and left just before Rogers and DeLuca arrived. They were supposed to find the gun and railroad me off the streets for a while. Bernie would be in charge of the case and he wouldn't hold me long enough for J.E. to get too nervous, but just long enough to be a stumbling block to finding T.M. But I figured the angle and ditched the heater before they got there. Which was too bad because that's when he decided to call you in, Riles. Nobody had an axe to grind with Steve Taylor or with Thelma, Bernie here just needed me looking in another direction. And murder gets so easy the second, third, or fourth time around. You knew Steve, Bill, from the days when he and I were still partners in the Parlor Detective Agency. And he knew you were a cop from bumping into you in those days, and from being one of your stoolies the last year or so. Your home phone number, the new one, in Bay Ridge, the one so new it isn't even listed in the phone book yet, was in his phone book. So when you showed up, and told him that you had to talk with him, or whatever diversion you used he naturally let you in.

"When did he realize, when you went for his gun? Or were you sly enough to make it look like some kind of routine inspection, so he'd never see it comin'? What's the matter, Bill, no tough guy answers now?"

Riles sat quietly on the floor where Cudge had deposited him. It was a strange feeling to be looking down on him after all our talks at the 83rd.

"I knew you were part of it when you slipped up over at Thelma's joint. It took me a while to remember but you said, 'What's a matter, Parker? No smart quotes now?' I was alone with Miss Collins when we used 'smart quotes.' You wouldn't have known about them unless you were one of the guys privy to the tapes that Bernie was very illegally having made here in Miss Collins' home. Another big mistake. I knew I was going in the right direction as soon as I saw that microphone planted. Fear is the only reason someone would have for doing that. And then giving so much time to get the money and make the drop. You wanted more listening time to see what I knew, if I was on to you yet. You outsmarted yourself, because at that point I didn't know a whole hell of a lot. You should have grabbed the cabbage and run, Bernie.

"I have to compliment you, Bill. That was a nice piece of driving over on Smith Street."

He looked amazed. It was an educated guess, really. I knew it had to be one of them and having ridden with Bernie for a few years I knew it sure as hell wasn't him behind that wheel.

"You stupid jerk!" Bernie screamed his best high pitch scream at Riles.

"Don't go givin' yourself too much credit, Bernie, you slipped up too."

"Yeah, Harry, when was that?"

"The second time you and Riles had me in for a ... chat. You said stop askin' questions about a bunch of stiffs that don't concern' ya. You were quite emphatic with the plural of the word stiffs. Yet as far as you should have known I was askin' about only one stiff, that being Steve. But because you were having me tailed you knew I was asking about Ruby, Phil, Rogers and DeLuca.

"You tried your damnedest for a fifth murder too, Bernie, let's not forget Cudge."

"Thanks, Harry." Cudge sounded truly thankful to be remembered as an attempted murder victim.

Charles began an extremely slow, almost undetectable back pedal from the room. "Don't go on my account, Charles." He stopped in his tracks. "You slipped up too. When you were waiting for me on my stoop, you said, 'Don't let me find out you were workin' on the Taylor murder case when you should be workin' for Mr. C.' Now if you and Bernie weren't in cahoots, how did you know I was on the Taylor case? How did you even know there was a Taylor case? And you had so much faith in Bernie's prediction that I couldn't solve the case you kept pressing me on, trying to prove your innocence. After all a guilty man wouldn't keep pressing for his own capture. Well, I'm afraid you tried much too hard, Charles." He tried to make a run for it but Cudge was quicker, grabbing, bending and holding his wrist behind his back. About a minute worth's of words was exchanged between them, too low for anyone else to hear.

"What did our not so silent butler have to say for himself, Cudge?" I inquired.

He took a look at Miss Collins. "Should I leave out all the words that ain't polite?"

"Yes."

"He didn't say nothin'."

"Poor T.M., betrayed by his own butler," I went on.

"Not me! I didn't kill anybody, Parker." The prison yard venom was back in his voice.

"No, that you didn't, Charlie boy. Not this time anyway. But you did deliver T.M. to his captors, didn't you? Knowing Bernie, I can take a real good guess on this one. He recognized you the night he came to sell Mr. Collins the tickets to the make believe Ball and to check things out for himself. Up to that point he only had what Ruby had told him and a vague plan. But when he saw you he realized he could threaten to tell the Collins family about your little axe wielding evening of a few years back if you didn't play along and that added tons of confidence to his idea. Correct?"

"Don't bother to deny it, Charles."

"Daddy!" screamed J.E. as T.M. entered the room with the able assistance of two of Quiggly's men. He was looking a hell of a lot worse for the wear. She ran to his side and actually allowed tears to ruin her expensive make up job. They gave each other a warm, hard, and probably very long overdue hug. The beauty of J.E. and the moment almost obliterated the horrors of the preceding days. The boys had taken T.M. to the hospital to make sure he was relatively okay, before bringing him home for the touching reunion and the grand finale.

"Baby," was all he said, but it said it all.

Bernie had been smug enough about my ineptness to hide T.M. in the same abandoned rooming house we used to deposit our stoolies in until things cooled off on the occasions we had worked together. I was surprised the rats hadn't eaten through his ropes and freed him before I got there.

"I didn't know about the finger, Mr. Collins, honest I swear I... " Charles began.

"Keep your trap shut, you idiot!" Bernie tried to cut in but Charles gave him his best eyes wide open axe wielding glare and went on.

"Honest, Mr. Collins, I didn't know they were going to hurt you."

"You helped them bring me to that ... place." He spoke with a low hatred in his voice that was more unforgiving than the loudest yell. "A single, narrow cot in the middle of a bare, frozen January room. An old, thin chenille bedspread with the fringe hanging all around is all there was to keep away the cold. And I clung to it like it was my mother comforting me from a little boy's bad dream, pulling it up tight all around, hoping that the roaches and the vermin didn't use the fringe as a ladder to get up into the bed. I tried so hard to speak but my mouth was so dry no words would come out."

"You were drugged, Mr. Collins." I attempted to explain his lost touch with reality.

"Ah, yes, Mr. Parker, that would account for my sometimes lazy, sometimes paranoid thinking. And the fact that some shadowy figure kept coming in the room would probably mean I was kept drugged wouldn't it, Mr. Parker?"

"Easier to keep you from complaining about the posh accommodations, Mr. Collins." It wasn't meant as a joke, more of an attempt to lighten his new reality of the situation.

"Couldn't you even have tried to escape, Father?" Janet's eyes were those of a little girl asking "why's the sky blue," or some other, equally innocuous question.

"My legs were weighted. I was unable to move them. It was as if your Aunt Maude was laying across them."

"Father!" She was back to her normal, very prim and proper, self.

"Oh, I hope I counted correctly on those toast orders," I said, trying to lighten the mood, but no one else was doing any eating.

It was a touching scene and I wondered if I could bother Charles for some of those gooey pastries before he had to leave but I figured it was too late when I saw that Quiggly was already cuffing the bracelets on him. What the hell, a little more French toast won't hurt. Cudge, Doc and John Divine joined me as everybody else was either celebrating or being arrested.

I looked at Bernie as Quiggly was going through his pockets.

"Why, Bernie?" was all I could come up with.

"What's a cop's pension get ya but a self-inflicted bullet on a lonely summer night?" came his almost whispered answer.

John Mason walked over in time to save me from becoming a murderer myself. Four people killed, one kidnapped, one attempted murder, because his pension wasn't going to be big enough! Mason stood between Bernie and me and said, "You know, I should be very angry with you, Mr. Parker."

"Oh, and why's that, Mr. Mason?" I said not too politely, still glaring over his shoulder at Bernie.

"By inviting me here today to witness this event you have precluded me from throwing my hat back in the prosecutorial ring, as it were. I would have loved to prosecute this matter."

"So sorry."

He smiled. "I wouldn't have missed it for the world." In another life he might have been an okay guy. I was glad I had made my deal with Divine about leaving the insider stuff on Mason and Collins out of his story in exchange for the exclusive on the kidnapping and murder cases. He hadn't really minded the trade off as much I'd figured. After all his story was on police corruption and he certainly got a whopper there. Wall Street, it seemed, could wait to be exposed - probably forever. I had considered letting him go with the insider info jazz, but was afraid it would bring old T.M. down hard. Not that I was so sure that that was a bad thing. But it wouldn't be good for business, clients being arrested with information I had uncovered during a case. Now that Mason was almost being human it seemed like an even better idea.

As Bernie was being led from the room I slipped my watch into his pocket. "Just the thing for keeping time in prison," I said, hoping it would add to his frustrations and bring closure to a part of my life at the same time.

The room was now empty of crooks. Well, Bernie, Riles and Charles had been disposed of. J.E. came over to me and brought her smiling face with her. She handed me a check for the remainder of my fee with a handsome bonus zeroed in on the end of it. T.M. had joined us at the French toast platters, from the way he was wolfing it down it was rather evident that Bernie and Riles had not been the best of hosts.

After we chowed down and said our good-byes to T.M. and J.E. we headed out to the street. John Divine had his own car and we waved goodbye at the sidewalk. I had asked him to return the money I had paid him for information, seeing as how we were both professional men, working the same case and all. He smiled and said something about padded expense accounts which I chose to ignore in light of the fact that J.E. was standing by the door not far from me.

Doc and Cudge climbed in the old Buick with me and I dropped them off at their homes. Cudge told us that there were two-hundred-thousand cubic feet of Indiana limestone used in the Empire State Building as he got out at his place. I pitied him the clean up chore he had ahead and drove off a little faster than usual before he thought to ask for our help.

Doc checked his watch as he got out. I envied him his correct time perfection as he said he could still catch his favorite music show on the radio.

I cruised on back toward my place, stopping to pick up the Eagle at the corner stand and milk and doughnuts at Whelan's. I parked two doors up from my abode and went on up to read in peace all about the case I had solved. Divine was a good man. I counted my name nine times in the lengthy article. Rogers, it seemed, would not only stay out of jail because of his decision to cooperate on the case but he would also be allowed to stay on the force, albeit on Staten Island. Like Napoleon to Elba.

I turned to the funny pages. Dick Tracy had just met a beautiful dame named Kiss Andtel and I knew even with the murder of one of his motorcycle patrolmen he was in for a better day than the ones I'd had lately. Actually, my biggest regret in the whole affair had been not inviting Thelma to be in on the finish. It was truly my shining moment.

There was a very loud knock, knock, knock at the door, and I opened it to an extremely excited Mr. Bellem.

"Mr. Parker, you must help me!" he implored. "I am having an affair with a married woman and ... and. ... Here, see for yourself."

He handed me a bunch of five word, very recognizable notes and said he would pay anything to find the author.

He must have thought I was crazy when I couldn't stop laughing.

38148968R00138

Made in the USA
Lexington, KY
04 May 2019